Dragon Village
GOLDEN APPLE

RONESA AVEELA

BENDIDEIA
PUBLISHING

Contents

Characters

Theo: Thirteen-year-old boy who has connections to Dragon Village.

Pavel: Theo's best friend who invents gadgets.

Diva: Samodiva girl who lives in Dragon Village. Diva's name means "wild." *Samodiva* means "Wild alone." From Bulgarian mythology, Samodivi were wild creatures who shied away from humans.

Baba Yaga: Witch from Slavic folklore who lives in a house with chicken feet.

Bendis: Thracian goddess of the moon, often said to be the mother of the Samodivi.

Bird of Paradise: Spirit birds, such as Sirin, Alkonost, and Gamayun.

Boo: A magpie.

Bor Stobor: A Karakonjul. *Bor* means pine in Bulgarian, and *stobor* is a strong person (strong like a big pine wood).

Celestial Turtle: A giant turtle from the mythologies of various cultures. It holds the world on its back.

Colobar (plural, Colobari): A priest of the god Tangra.

Dracoville: A nickname Pavel gave Theo, combining his dragon and Samodiva heritages.

Drakus: An Oupir (vampire).

Firebird: In Slavic mythology, a bird that can be both a blessing and a curse. Its feathers glow brightly, and some say the bird can see the future.

Hala: Lamia and Zmey's mother. Female dragon who is associated with the wind and bringing storms.

Harpy: Half-woman, half-bird creature from Thrace and found in Greek mythology.

Ispolin (plural, Ispolini): Bulgarian word for "giants."

Jabalaka: The Keeper of Secrets. A man Lamia turned into a frog creature. *Jaba* is the Bulgarian word for "frog."

Jega: A Kuker (mummer) who wields fire. The word *jega* means "hot" in Bulgarian.

Karakonjul: Half-man, half-horse creature.

Kikimora: Creature who lives in the marsh, where she brews beer.

Knights of Darkness: Knights of Light who were corrupted by Zlo.

Knights of Light: Zmey's special guards who remained faithful.

Konedrakon (plural, Konedrakoni): A fictional mythical creature that is a combination of horse and dragon. *Kone* is "horse" in Bulgarian, and *drakon* is "dragon."

Kosara: Guardian of the Znahar Tree.

Kotka: Baba Yaga's flying cat. *Kotka* is the Bulgarian word for "cat."

Kuker (plural, Kukeri): A man who wears animal skins and huge bells that scare evil spirits. The tradition dates back to Thracian times.

Lamia: Zmey's sister. Female dragon with three dog-like heads. She is cruel and brings hail to destroy crops, as well as stopping the flow of water.

Lora: Drakus' wife.

Lord Vodnik: Leader of the water creatures.

Lucky: One of Lord Vodnik's male water buffaloes.

Magda: Zunitza's sister.

Mora (plural, Mori): A type of demon that causes nightmares.

Mraz: The oldest of the Kukeri brothers. The Bulgarian word is for "cold."

Nav (plural, Navi): A demon that looks like a bird with a distorted infant's head.

Nia: Theo's twin sister.

Oupir: A type of Bulgarian vampire.

Radan: A warrior, Lord Zlo's second-in-command.

Samodiva (plural, Samodivi): Woodland nymph in Bulgarian lore. You may be more familiar with one of their other names: Veelas, like in the Harry Potter stories.

Sava: Diva's oldest sister.

Shar: Theo's deer companion. *Shar* means "colorful" in Bulgarian.

Sirin: One of the "birds of paradise," half-women, half bird. She sang beautiful songs that made listeners forget everything.

Sitara: Blacksmith. Former Vurkolak (werewolf) who once guarded one of Lamia's souls.

Sly: A Vodnik, friendly toward Theo.

Struma: Spirit of a woman built into a bridge wall.

Sur: Diva's deer companion. *Sur* means "gray" in Bulgarian.

Tangra: Thracian god of light and the sun.

Ula: Diva's sister.

Vodnik (plural, Vodni): Slavic water creature that looks like an old man or a frog-like creature.

Vurkolak: Bulgarian word for "werewolf."

Water Bull: Demonic creature, part bull, part fish, part human, that lives in Rabisha Lake.

Whirl: Pavel's deer companion.

Youda (plural, Youdi): Evil Samodiva who lives in forests and mountains. She has the power of witchcraft.

Zima: A Kuker who has the power of freezing. The word *zima* means "winter" in Bulgarian.

Zlo: Lamia's lord and mentor. The word in Bulgarian means "bad" or "evil."

Zmey: Theo's birth father. Villages throughout Bulgaria have invisible patrons who protect their villages.

Zunitza: A Samodiva. Theo's birth mother. The word comes from *zuna*, the Bulgarian for "rainbow."

Glossary

Chamber Room: Room in the castle where the Golden Apple is hidden.

Cherna Mountain: *Cherna* is the Bulgarian word for "black." This is where the dragon castle is found.

Chutura: An old Bulgarian word for "mortar."

Cold Marsh: Home of the Vodni, Jabalaka, and Kikimora.

Devil's Throat: A cave in the western Rhodope Mountains in Bulgaria, said to be the entrance to Hades.

Dracophone: Pavel's invention to call home to Selo.

Forest of Souls: The place where the souls of Dragon Village's ancestors reside in globes.

Forest of Whispering Bells: Forest where Baba Yaga lives. The bells jingle when someone approaches.

Golden Apple: In Slavic folklore, a fruit that has an association with the Firebird.

Kaleto: The Forgotten Land, home of the Ispolini. In Bulgarian, the name means "fortress."

Lamia's Bible: A book that contains secrets about those living in Dragon Village.

Magura Cave: A cave in northern Bulgaria where prehistoric paintings have been found. The cave is near Rabisha Lake.

Ouroboros: A snake or dragon swallowing its tail and forming a circle, symbolizing infinity.

Paveltron: Pavel's multi-purpose gadget.

Rabisha Lake: A freshwater lake in northern Bulgaria that legends say is the home of the Water Bull.

Rhyton: A conical-shaped drinking vessel.

Selo: Fictitious place along the Black Sea. Bulgarian word for "village."

Tililei Forest: Forest teeming with demons.

Vida: Village where Youdi and Sitara live.

Zmeykovo: Bulgarian name for "Dragon Village." Mystical land where mythological creatures live. Said to be at the end of the world.

Znahar Tree: A fictitious World Tree connecting the three realms: heavens, earth, and underworld.

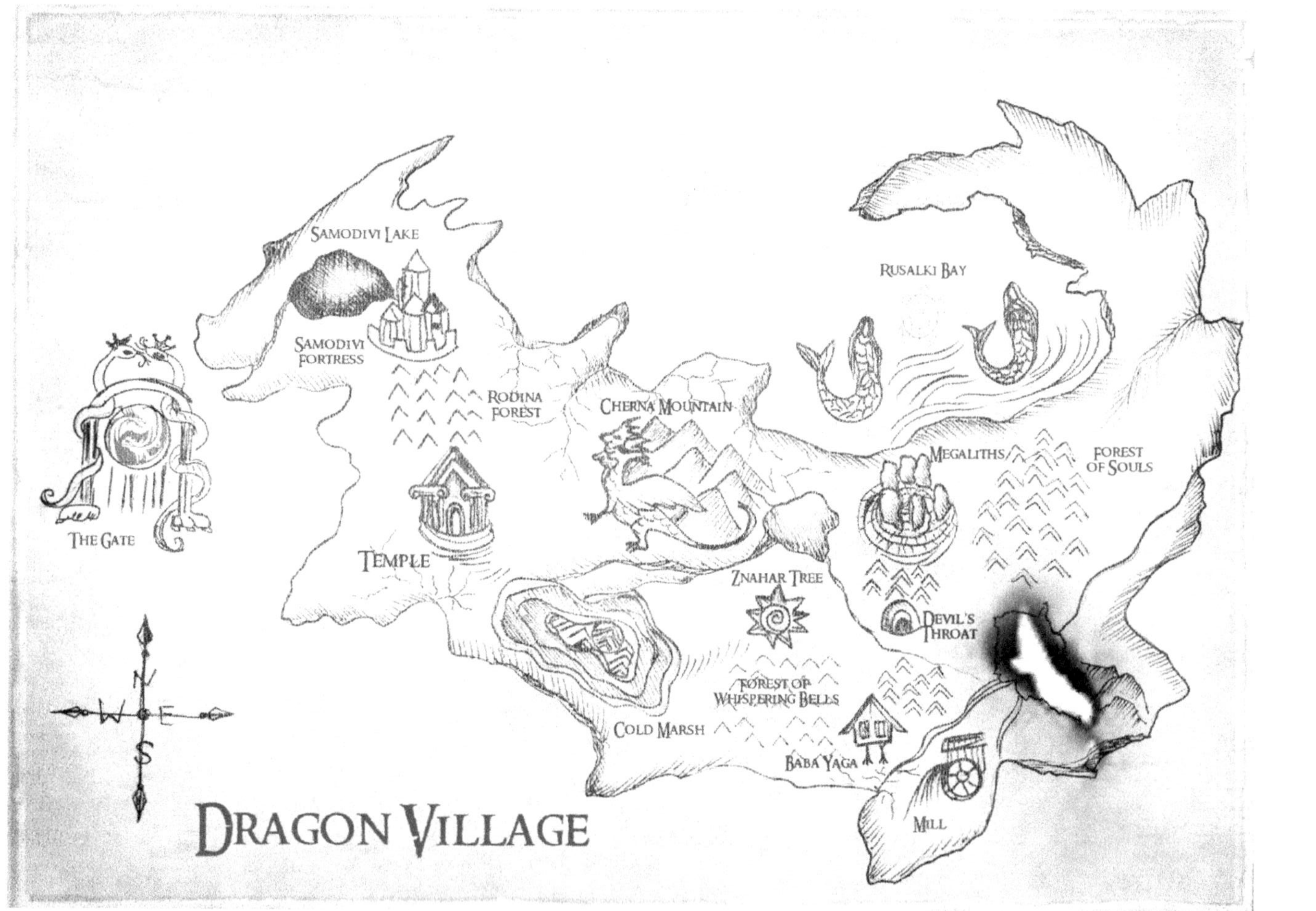

SAMODIVI LAKE
SAMODIVI FORTRESS
RODINA FOREST
CHERNA MOUNTAIN
RUSALKI BAY
MEGALITHS
FOREST OF SOULS
THE GATE
TEMPLE
ZNAHAR TREE
DEVIL'S THROAT
FOREST OF WHISPERING BELLS
COLD MARSH
BABA YAGA
MILL
DRAGON VILLAGE

Chapter 1
The Light Within

JULY 10

THE MAJESTIC STATUE of the two dragons craved to reveal its secrets. Theo could sense the power pulsing within it. Zmey and Lamia's parents kneeled on the back of a huge turtle, the Celestial Turtle, the Mother of the Universe. Theo had discovered that piece of information while he scoured the castle's scant library. The first time he'd seen this statue in the small ballroom, he'd marveled at how in love the couple looked.

Cradled between the dragons were two eggs. An engraving had been etched into each with precious metals, silver on Zmey's white egg and gold on Lamia's golden one. The design was of an ouroboros, not the familiar snake swallowing its tail, but a dragon formed the circle of eternal life. Like the dragon couple, love shone on the faces of these dragon etchings. A special bond had existed between Zmey and Lamia even before they hatched.

A bittersweet feeling overwhelmed Theo every time he came into this room. So much love had turned to hate. The animosity was enough to cause one sibling to attempt to murder the other. For what? Jealousy? Power? Pride? Compulsion? He didn't know the entire story about what had caused a rift between his father and aunt. Theo had always thought nothing could come between twins.

"What are you trying to tell me?" he asked the dragons.

He'd felt the pull of the statue so strongly these past couple of days, drawing him here to stand for hours, staring at the once-happy family. Today was different. The statue silently compelled him to touch the ouroboros engraving on Zmey's egg.

Theo hesitated as he reached out his hand. *What's going to happen if I do?*

In the past, strange things had occurred when he'd touched magical items. A marble dragon had softened in Selo. And in Zmeykovo, a globe in the secret garden had shown him a vision of his upcoming battle with Lamia.

What revelation will I receive today?

He lowered his hand to graze the surface of the etching. A chill raced up his arm, and he shuddered. A mystical energy beyond his understanding spread throughout his body.

Then a voice hummed in Theo's mind. "*Look at me!*"

He raised his head to the dragons. Four ruby eyes pierced his brain like a burning sword.

The floor dissolved into a mist, leaving him drifting in nothingness. From the direction of the statue, a pinprick of light appeared. It swirled, slowly at first, but picked up speed until it grew larger and brighter, swallowing him.

Within the midst of the light, a calming, but authoritative voice like none he'd heard before spoke. *"Theo, the fate of your father and Zmeykovo is in your hands. Be strong. Use your mind but listen to your heart. Don't be afraid. Fear limits us, and we cannot move forward."* The voice faded, but left Theo with its whispered parting words. *"He who has light within himself will tear apart the darkness."*

The light vanished as quickly as it had appeared. Theo discovered himself standing by the statue, his hand still upon the etching on Zmey's egg. He swayed when he tried to move, so he leaned his head against the cool marble until the dizziness receded.

No one else was in the room, so the voice had to have come from the statue … or the egg. He glanced at the dragons' eyes again. Once more, they were lifeless.

Theo hadn't been terrified this time when a dragon statue spoke to him. When Zmey's figure back in Selo had done that, Theo thought he was going crazy.

Maybe I shouldn't keep touching dragon statues. He laughed nervously as he rubbed his aching head.

But at least he'd received an answer, even though it was another riddle. What did the voice mean about the light and the darkness? If anyone knew, it would be Zmey.

Theo hurried to his father's room and peered through the door, which had been left open a crack. A subdued aroma of herbs and incense permeated the dim bedroom. The scents were meant for healing and comfort, but they provided little solace for Theo. How could he relax when his father, the dragon king, lay shivering under sweat-soaked covers?

If Death were more than an imaginary being, he'd be standing in the corner waiting to take Zmey to the otherworld. Actually, the Forest of Souls, Theo corrected himself. That's where his mother's soul resided, and he assumed his father would go there, too, when he died. Theo locked his arms around his chest as if trying to keep his racing heart from exploding out of his chest. He examined every inch of the room. In this magical land of Zmeykovo, he couldn't be sure the creature Death didn't actually exist and was waiting nearby to seize the dragon king.

Zmey groaned in his sleep. Theo entered the room and approached the bed. He rested his hand on his father's sunken grayish cheek. The once powerful man looked so small, cocooned within pillows and quilts. Gold thread embroidered into the olive-green fabric remained the only indication that the man lying there held a royal status.

I don't know how Dad has survived like this for the past week. Magda brought him back from certain death, but it's not enough. I need to recover Zmey's ouroboros belt. That Lamia ... Theo clenched his fists.

His father stirred. Theo flexed his fingers and rubbed gentle circles on Zmey's cheek. "Shh. Sorry I disturbed you."

"Theo?" Zmey blinked and squinted in the candle's glow.

"I'm here."

With rapid, shallow breaths, Zmey twisted his head in Theo's direction.

"Let me help you." Theo raised his father to a sitting position and adjusted the pillows and blankets to secure him.

"Thank you." Zmey coughed through hoarse words. Finally, he patted the bed. "Come closer. We need to talk."

Afraid of hurting Zmey, Theo hesitated before sitting on the edge of the bed. He picked up his father's hand and gently squeezed it. A faint, but steady pulse beat against Theo's palm.

"Son, every day I don't have my belt my strength grows weaker."

"I'll save you." Theo held back the tears, wanting to be strong for his father. "I'll get your belt back. I'll—"

"No, Theodore." Zmey shook his head. "I know you're doing everything you can to help me, but Lamia's too strong. And with Zlo's help … I fear for your safety if you go up against them again." He closed his eyes while he swallowed several times.

Theo poured cold water into a rhyton on the bedside table and handed Zmey the drink.

After taking small sips and licking his parched lips, Zmey rasped, "Before I leave you, I need to tell you something important. Since you're my heir, I must make sure you're ready to rule."

While Zmey stopped to sip more water, Theo's mind raced with thoughts of what kind of task his father would demand of him. Didn't an heir in fairy tales slay a dragon to prove his worthiness? Theo had already done that. It wasn't his fault his aunt, the cursed Lamia, had been revived. Or maybe it was. If Theo hadn't returned to Zmeykovo, Lord Zlo wouldn't have been able to bring Lamia back from the dead. But then, if Theo hadn't come, he would never have been able to rescue his father either.

As if reading Theo's mind, Zmey continued, "First, let me say that I believe in you and know you'll be a worthy leader. I'm confident you'll rescue Zmeykovo from Zlo, and I believe there's still a chance you can save my sister."

Theo grunted. He had no desire to save Lamia. She'd proven she had no love for her own brother when she'd stolen his belt and left him to die in the bowels of the earth. If it hadn't been for Zunitza's care, her spirit remaining with Zmey the entire time, he would have died before Theo had a chance to rescue him. No, Lamia deserved whatever punishment Theo could dole out to her.

"But that's not what I need to tell you," Zmey continued. "As ruler of Zmeykovo, I have an obligation to my beloved residents to take care of their security, prosperity, and future. It's important that you know and live our sacred creed." Zmey paused and spoke as if reciting a long-memorized quote, "He who has light within himself will tear apart the darkness."

"What?" Theo jerked backward. "I … I heard that already today. That's why I came here. What does it mean?" Was the universe telling him that everything would be fine, and he would succeed if he believed in himself?

"It's what I was taught when I was trained to control my powers and learn how to rule." Zmey coughed. His next words were weak, and he spoke them with effort. "It comes from the book *Lodge of Light and Lodge of Darkness*. You must search for the light of Tangra and let it guide you. Light is the highest level of purity. It's what will make you a strong, honorable leader. This is what you'll need in your fight against Zlo and his darkness. You must discover the light within yourself and carry it with you."

Theo didn't understand what his father was saying, but he nodded vigorously.

Pleading with troubled eyes, Zmey reached for Theo's hand. "Promise me you'll always care for our people and land the way I have. I've put them before my own needs."

"I will." Theo choked on his words.

He could no longer hold back the tears, and they jiggled down his cheeks. His father couldn't die yet. Theo didn't know if he was ready to take on such a big responsibility or if he was capable of honoring the promise he'd just made.

How am I going to manage this?

He had two homes. Zmeykovo and Selo. The moment he'd found his father in the prison, Theo had stopped thinking about this land as Dragon Village. Now, to him, it was Zmeykovo, the name those who lived here called it.

But how could he abandon his human mother and his sister, Nia, in Selo? They needed him too, and he had promised to keep them safe.

"I'll find Lamia," he said with a shaky voice. "I'll take your belt back from her and save you. You have to hold on and be strong, Father."

Zmey continued as if he hadn't heard Theo, "We haven't had much time to talk about Zmeykovo. I don't have time to teach you how to use your gifts and the powers you inherited from your mother and me. There's so much to learn about how to control them, about being a dragon, but you're like your mother, smart and good. I know you'll find a way."

"I will. I will." Theo rested his head in his hands.

"Find Jabalaka," Zmey said. "He's a good teacher. He has a wealth of knowledge and more books than you'd ever be able to read in a human lifetime."

Theo tightened his grip on his forehead, and his body went cold. *Zmey doesn't remember that Jabalaka died! And that Lamia burned his library!*

"Oh, Father!" Theo gently wrapped his arms around Zmey's frail body. "I will. Don't worry. I'll learn everything I need to know. I've read a book about Zmeykovo's history and its secrets and hidden knowledge."

"Good, good." Zmey patted Theo's back.

After releasing his father, Theo wiped away his tears using the back of his hand.

"There's more," Zmey said. "Learn all you can about Tangra, our sun god, and the Znahar Tree." Zmey closed his eyes. His words began to slur and were broken as he rambled from one subject to another. "Humans expelled us. Called us evil. Black forces. Samodiva. Magda. Trust her. Zunitza." And more words Theo couldn't decipher.

"Yes, I'll learn." Theo leaned forward and kissed his father's cheek. "I'll let you rest now. I'll find Magda, so she can give you medicine."

"No, wait." Zmey fluttered his eyes open. "I need to tell you more. This key …" With a shaking hand, he reached under his nightshirt and displayed a key on a golden chain. Interlocking loops, the symbol of the Celestial Turtle, embellished the stem. "This unlocks a place only the ruler has access to. It will be yours when I'm gone. I need to show you the Chamber …"

Zmey broke out into a coughing fit, and sweat poured down his face. He rasped out words between breaths. "Zunitza, my love. I'm coming."

Theo touched Zmey's forehead. It was scorching.

"Magda!" Theo ran to the door and threw it open. Where was she? She hadn't been anywhere near the room when Theo arrived, and she was supposed to be taking care of Zmey.

"I'm here." A thin figure appeared from a dark corridor, light from a lamp casting shadows on her pale, expressionless face. In the dim light, Magda looked like the incarnation of Death that Theo feared would take his father away, but, for now, she was Zmey's only hope of survival.

"Help Zmey, please!"

Magda rushed to Zmey's side. "Shh. Shh." She removed a box from a drawer in the nightstand, selected something, and waved it under Zmey's nose. "Breathe. These dry herbs will calm you."

Slowly, Zmey's hacking cough subsided.

Magda withdrew a pinch more of herbs from the box, put them into a small bag, and dunked them in a container of water. She lifted Zmey's head. "Drink this. It'll help you rest."

After he did, she lowered him so he could sleep. "Theo, could you get the robe and belt that are in the cupboard? Zmey likes to hold them when he gets like this."

"I didn't mean to upset him."

Magda shook her head. "It wasn't you. It just happens." She held out her hand. "The robe and belt, please?"

Theo opened the door and discovered two garments. One was the robe Magda had mentioned. He caressed the silky white fabric. It reflected the dim light in the room. The material was so delicate he believed the stories that said Samodivi wore clothing made from moonbeams. Patterns on the robe were embroidered in red along the neckline and cuffs. The images represented nature and the connection with the land: trees, animals, herbs, and more.

They told a story about Zmeykovo and the lives of the Samodivi, their bravery and the role they played as protectors of the land, as well as their goddess and her temple.

Next to the robe, a dress covered with golden coins, looking like scales, shimmered in the soft candlelight. The flexible material flowed to the bottom of the cupboard. Theo glanced down the length of the dress. The golden color transitioned into deeper hues of copper and bronze toward the bottom.

"It's beautiful," he said as he handed the robe to Magda. "The dress is, too."

"They're both part of Zunitza's wedding ensemble, an outfit worthy of our queen, leader of the Samodivi." She pressed her lips into a tight smile.

Theo looked at the wedding dress again. It certainly was worthy of his mother. Young women in his village had similar wedding dresses, but the gold coins on theirs only covered the bib. They were sewn on to represent a dragon's scales. Even though the village had rituals to protect girls from being abducted by a dragon, they still dressed as if they were dragon brides. Zmeykovo's Samodiva queen was a true dragon bride.

"Please give me the belt, too," Magda said. "It'll bring Zmey's fever down more quickly."

"I didn't see one." Theo went to the cupboard to check again. "Nope, no belt, only a robe and dress."

Magda scowled. "Diva was looking at the belt earlier. She must have stolen it."

"Why would she do that?"

"Let's leave so your father can rest. No need to upset him further." Outside Zmey's chambers, Magda said, "Whoever took the belt knows about its power. It's even more powerful than the robe. If it wasn't Diva, then you have another thief here. When you're destined to rule, everyone is a potential enemy. Friends turn on you."

"But not Diva?" Doubt crept into Theo's mind.

Diva had enjoyed the cheers of the people when Theo had brought his father home. Did she want to rule Zmeykovo?

Had Zmey, in his ramblings, said a *Samodiva* practiced black forces or had he said *Diva* did? Zmey's words were so slurred, it was difficult to tell. But he had also said to trust Magda, hadn't he?

"Let me help you find the truth." Magda hugged Theo. "I've kept your father safe. I'll do the same for you. We're family, after all. I love you like a son."

Chills crept over Theo. Was it from Magda's touch or the thought of Diva betraying him?

Chapter 2
Magda's Story of Woe

MAGDA LED THEO to a terrace that overlooked a flower garden. Stone pathways crisscrossed in many directions, with benches and roses of every color imaginable nestled along both sides. Landmarks scattered throughout the area were a photographer's dream setting. Closest to the terrace, a trellis with a white picket fence gate wore a cluster of full red blossoms like a crown. In the center of the garden, a fountain spouted water that flowed down into three successive scalloped basins. Farther away, roses crowded around a gazebo like an assembly waiting for a festivity's entertainment to begin.

But what caught Theo's attention the most were beautiful golden roses that twisted around a marble pedestal in the center of the terrace. Their translucent petals captured the sun's rays, making them sparkle and glow like gems. He stepped closer and lightly traced his fingers along a silky petal, almost afraid it would disintegrate at his touch. A sweet aroma of honeysuckle drifted around the flowers.

Magda came to stand beside him. "Zunitza planted those on her wedding day. Roses were her favorite flower. She used to make her own perfume and water."

"They're … amazing."

"They are. Everything about your mother was … amazing. Her looks. Her personality. Her life. It made me feel … so … so invisible." Magda let out a long sigh as she sat on a bench. Shadows from the balcony above the terrace hid her face from Theo, but not her emotions.

Theo joined her and took her hand in his. "But you're identical twins. You look the same, and you seem … nice, too."

"I'm sorry." Magda dabbed at her eyes with the edge of her sleeve. "I brought you here to make you feel better, not to talk about myself."

"No, please. Tell me about it if it helps."

She locked eyes with him. A deep sadness and something more, like a hunger, shone in her eyes. Her face had softened from the harsh, stern image she normally presented to the world. Even her way of dressing had changed from the goth-like attire Theo had first seen her wear. Earthy tones now draped over her body, and soft-looking gloves hid the golden snake bracelets that spiraled around his aunt's wrists. A heart-shaped pendant graced her throat, and she'd allowed soft curls to frame her face, rather than her former snakelike braids.

A gentle breeze blew the scent of Magda's perfume his way. It smelled of honeysuckle, reminding Theo of the aroma that surrounded his mother. But it also held a hint of roses.

For the moment, Theo could believe that Magda was his mother's twin.

"Are you sure?" Magda asked.

Theo nodded. He'd heard so many tragic stories from people he'd met in Zmeykovo. His Vodnik friend Sly. The blacksmith Sitara. Struma the ghost. Even the strange bird-like creature Kikimora had sorrow in her life. He wasn't quite sure he believed the witch Baba Yaga yet when she cried, "Woe is me," but the others had true tales that made his heart break. It was too much for someone so young like him to take in, so he kept their pains locked away until the day he became ruler and could rightfully make amends for them.

He had failed Jabalaka and Zima. Theo couldn't save either of the Kukeri from death. He didn't want to endure another loss. Why not add Magda to that list of those he might be able to help one day? She didn't give him warm vibes, but he hadn't really offered her a chance. Now was the time to at least give her the opportunity to tell her story.

"Thank you." Magda squeezed his hand. "Zunitza and I were close as children, always sharing everything. She was outgoing, and people flocked to her. They allowed me to participate in activities because she demanded it, but that didn't mean they were nice to me when she wasn't looking."

"Uh-huh." Theo understood that story. It sounded a lot like him and Pavel—at least in Selo. Here in Zmeykovo, things had been reversed, and Pavel still sulked about it from time to time. It's not as if Theo *liked* being the center of attention. He much preferred to be a follower. Or did he? He had been annoyed with Zima for always expecting everyone to do things the Kuker's way, and had been pleased the one time Zima had stayed behind. This allowed Theo to make the decisions for his friends.

"Even our parents preferred Zunitza." Magda stopped to sniff.

"Huh?" Those words brought Theo out of his introspection. He should be listening to his aunt, not thinking about his own problems. "Oh, that's terrible."

"I know." Magda blinked as if to regain her thoughts. "I'd often overhear them talk about how Zunitza was their joy. They called her a beauty, a vibrant, tender lily."

"I'm so sorry you had to hear something like that, but …" Theo paused. He didn't want to say something in the wrong way to upset Magda. "Do you think maybe you heard it out of context? They may have said something about your abilities before that, something that you missed."

"No." She shook her head. "I heard much more than that on many occasions."

Theo shivered. The thought about curiosity killing the cat popped into his head. Was Magda a snoop? Intentionally trying to find out things about people? No, he shouldn't think that way. She had just been a child at the time, after all, hadn't she? Children were naturally curious.

"Unlike Zunitza, I was shy. It was difficult to open up to people. They called me moody or stuck-up because I kept my thoughts to myself. It made me resentful of the affection they showed to Zunitza." Magda rose and paced the terrace. She stopped and turned to Theo, a hard look on her face. "Worse, they said I was cold, jealous, and demanding, all because I wanted a little attention. So, in time, that's what I became. I'd show them I didn't need their love. I had my brains, and that was better than beauty any day."

The softness Theo had witnessed in Magda's features had vanished. Hard, cold anger glared at him. He stared at her with his mouth agape. He certainly wasn't going to tell Magda if she looked that way at people in the past it was no wonder they said the things they did about her.

"Forgive me. I didn't mean to scare you." She lowered her head. "You think you've overcome your past and moved on, but it's just buried deep and surfaces when you focus on it again."

"I … I understand. It's okay. We all have things that trigger our anger." Theo thought about Baba Yaga's continued betrayals, and how mad that made him. Sometimes, his feelings weren't righteous anger. They were selfish.

Magda sat next to him again. "You do, don't you?"

Theo nodded. His own emotions started to bubble to the surface. He couldn't stop thinking about Diva's possible betrayal. "I have to ask Diva if she took the belt. And why."

Magda grabbed his shoulders. She hissed, "Trust me, Theo. You don't want to do that. If she's guilty, it'll only inform her that you're aware of her deceit. That would escalate matters. She might harm you … or even Zmey. I have ways to discover the truth. Please let me handle it."

"O-okay."

Theo didn't want to have to confront Diva. What if Magda was wrong? Accusing Diva of theft and being power hungry would damage their friendship. He'd already messed up enough with Pavel and had to solve the problems between them. Without Diva's support, Theo would be completely lost. She helped him see things rationally. But what if it had all been a ploy for power?

"Wise choice." Magda released him and pressed her lips together before she picked up her life story. "People here thwarted me in other ways, too. I wanted to become a Colobar."

"What's that?"

"It's a high honor for those of royal blood or high social position." Magda looked at Theo as if daring him to contest her worthiness. When he nodded, she continued, "Colobari are priests of our sun god, Tangra. I studied to be the first woman to hold that position."

"Wow!"

"Yes, wow, indeed." Magda's face lit up. "I studied for years. I excelled at everything I learned and thought being selected into the sacred organization was a certainty, but …"

"But …" Theo prompted, but Magda remained silent. "Did … did my mother have something to do with stopping you?" He held his breath, not wanting the answer to be yes.

Magda jumped up. "Oh, why torture myself about it again? What's done is done. It doesn't matter what happened. But I wasn't allowed that honor." She paced the terrace again, mumbling and clenching her fists.

"For what it's worth, I'm sorry."

Magda stared at Theo. A strange, almost regretful look passed over her face. Finally, in a low voice, she said, "Thank you. I should get back to see if Zmey's resting. I've been away for too long."

With that, she rushed back into the castle.

Theo wasn't ready to return. Magda had given him much to think about. He strolled over to the gazebo, inhaling the rose scents as he went. It calmed his raging soul somewhat, but confusion still clouded his mind.

"*Mom,*" he thought as he sat on the gazebo bench, "*are you here?*"

Zunitza didn't respond. Perhaps she was watching over Zmey while Magda was away. Theo hoped his mother told his father to hang on, that it wasn't time for him to join her yet, that Theo still needed him.

He waited a while longer, listening to the birds and watching the butterflies and bees flit around the flowers. Then he tried again. "*If you're here, Mom, will you tell me if you had anything to do with Magda not being able to become a Colobar?*"

"*I'm here, my beloved son.*" A gentle breeze ruffled Theo's hair. "*I don't know what Magda told you, but no, I never wanted any harm to come to her. I tried to make her feel happy and wanted. Despite things that happened, I never stopped loving her.*"

"*What happened? Why is she so filled with anger?*"

Zunitza sighed. "*I cannot enter Magda's mind and see or feel the things she does. We each believe truths about our own life, even if no one else sees their reality that way. All I can say is what I felt and what I saw. Magda let negativity consume her. It made her bitter and vengeful. She had so much goodness, but she repressed it. I tried to help, but it only made matters worse.*"

"*Thank you. I'll try to be more understanding of her.*" Theo thought how much Magda's story was probably like Lamia's. Zmey, and even Lamia herself, had talked about how the two of them had once been close. Lamia blamed the distance on Zunitza, saying she stole Zmey's love. But Lamia didn't seem to understand that Zmey loved them both, even now.

Scratching and shuffling came from under the gazebo. Theo put his hand onto the hilt of the sword that he always carried with him now. He focused on the noise. It sounded like an animal settling into a burrow. Probably a groundhog. He'd seen them crawl out from under a shed before. A nice home to keep them dry when it rained.

He turned his thoughts back to his own problems. "I can't believe Diva would try to take control of the kingdom." Speaking the words out loud felt like making it truer than having the words pounding against his brain, and Theo wished he'd kept silent.

"Why lovely Samodiva do that?" a voice under the gazebo responded.

"Who's there?" Theo jumped up and peered over the edge. The voice had sounded familiar, and only one creature he knew called Diva the lovely Samodiva. "Sly, is that you?"

"Yes, it's Sly. I here."

The Vodnik crawled from beneath the gazebo. Dirt and flower petals covered him.

"Why are you hiding under there?" Theo asked.

"Sly not hiding. I sleeping. Busy busy. Back and forth all day."

"Busy, huh? Come up here and tell me about it. I've missed you, my friend."

"Oh no no. Sly have big mouth. I can't talk now. Gotta run." The Vodnik scrambled through rose bushes. "Ow, ow, ow. Look what my King do now. I hurt."

"I'm sorry. Please don't leave. Stay and talk with me." Theo went down to untangle Sly from the thorns. "I won't make you tell me what you're so secretive about. I-I could use a friend right now."

"Sly friend?" The Vodnik's big bulging eyes seemed to pop out of his green head even more. He tugged on his long beard, scattering dirt and petals.

"Of course, you're a friend. You're a good friend. You've helped us so much."

"Okay, Sly stay, but my King promise not to make Sly break his promises?"

Theo made an "X" on his chest. "Cross my heart."

"I not understand, my King."

Theo laughed, and it felt good to be amused. "It just means I won't make you break your promises."

"Good. Sly get in big big trouble if I break promises." He scrambled up the steps and settled onto a bench.

Theo looked at the Vodnik for a while, not sure where to begin. The silence didn't seem to bother Sly. He sat quietly, stretching out his webbed fingers and toes, apparently captivated by them. Something was different about Sly, but Theo couldn't quite put his finger on what it was. He seemed more confident, chattier.

That was it!

"Sly," Theo almost shouted, "has someone been teaching you to speak better?"

"Speak better?" Sly tilted his head. "My King say strange things."

How do I make him understand? Theo thought. "You use more words now when you talk. And you use them better. You used to say 'me' when you talked about yourself. Now you say 'I,' which is correct. Has someone been correcting you when you say things?"

Sly jumped up and down on the bench. "Oh oh oh, my King, you promised not to make me break my promises!"

"I-I didn't intend to." Theo tugged at his hair. This was not going the way he wanted. "I didn't ask you what was keeping you busy. I didn't know asking you how you speak was making you break a promise. I'm sorry, again."

"Okay." Sly settled down on the bench. "Too much danger for Sly to tell anyone."

"Would it be okay if I tell you things that are bothering me?" Theo asked. "You can just listen. That won't be making you break any promises, right?"

"Yes, my King. Sly can listen."

Theo poured out his heart. He told Sly about how deathly ill his father was without the belt that Lamia had stolen. How he now wasn't sure he could trust Diva or even Pavel for that matter, since his best friend continued to side with Diva on all matters. How Magda was befriending Theo, but he wasn't sure how much he could trust his aunt either. But mostly, he talked about how inadequate he felt, sitting around doing nothing to make things better.

"So, there you have it. What do you think of all that? How can I make things right with everyone?"

"Sly cannot help, but I know someone who can."

"Really?" Theo leaned closer. "Who?"

"My King!" Sly screeched. "You break promise again! Sly cannot tell you." With that, the Vodnik scrambled down the steps and disappeared among the rose bushes.

Theo sat with his mouth open. *What in the world was* that *all about?*

Chapter 3
Visit from the Colobari

BEFORE RETURNING TO TRYING to find a way to retrieve Zmey's ouroboros belt, Theo stopped to check on how his father was doing. The massive wooden door to Zmey's room was closed. On the panels, the two crowned dragons on opposite sides of the Tree of Life appeared to be standing guard to prevent Theo from entering.

What's going on? Magda always leaves the door open a crack. My father didn't ... Theo couldn't say the word. He pressed his ear to the door. Muted male voices came from within. He caught a few words spoken a little louder as if in anger: *golden apple, trust, test, Tangra.*

"Theo!" Magda whispered behind him. "What are you doing? Get away from there."

He jumped and twisted around. "Who's in there? Why aren't you with Zmey?"

"The Colobari have come to consult with your father."

"What could be so important that they'd disturb a man on his deathbed?"

"That's not for you to know." She grabbed hold of his shirt sleeve and dragged him away from the door.

"But you know, don't you?"

Magda paled. "No, why would you say that? It's only a matter for the priests to discuss with your father, the king."

"Okay. I wasn't going to listen to their conversation. I only thought something had happened to my father." Theo released her grasp from his shirt. "Will you tell me about them, the Colobari? You said you studied to be one."

"I can't. It's a sacred organization."

"Please. There must be something you can say. I'm sure the people of Zmeykovo know about the men." Theo pleaded with his eyes. He'd often made his human mother cave in on her resolve with that look, like a wide-eyed puppy dog.

Magda let out an exasperated breath. "Fine."

She led him to a bench under a window. Trickles of sunlight seeped in through the stained glass and created figures of dancing dragons on the floor.

"I already told you they are priests of Tangra," she said as she sat. "He's our supreme god, so it's a great honor to be selected to minister to him."

"Yes, I've seen him," Theo said. "He helped make the dome that protects Kosara and the Znahar Tree."

"You are indeed blessed to have been in his presence." Magda looked Theo up and down, with what he thought was admiration—and envy. She spoke her next words so softly Theo wasn't sure he heard them correctly. "Maybe there's more to you than I thought."

"What did you say?"

She held up her hand. "Nothing. Colobar means 'little dragon.' They are—"

"Zmeykovo has more dragon people?"

"Yes, of course." Magda snorted. "Did you think your family was the only one?"

Theo felt his face heat up. "Um, yah, kinda."

"There are lots of dragon people, here and in your world."

A tingling sensation rippled through Theo's body. He wasn't alone. Other people, maybe even in Selo, had dragon blood. He wondered if there was a way he could tell or find them, maybe bring them to Zmeykovo someday.

Do they feel awkward like me? Do they have an overwhelming desire to fly? Do—?

"Theo?" Magda snapped her fingers in front of his face. "Come back to me."

"Sorry. I was just thinking—"

"Yes, about the other dragon people, I'm sure."

He nodded. "Can you tell me anything about the ones from the human world?"

"A little," she said. "Your history and ours are intertwined."

She sat without speaking for a while, half-closing her eyes and breathing deeply as if putting herself into a trance. Her voice was low when she began. "They called it the time when nature rebelled against humans. Thousands, perhaps millions of years ago, a cataclysmic event sent humans, unlike those you know, scurrying deep into the mountains, down, down, down through caves, so far that the air was hot and scorching. And they lived there for generations. It was also at this time that Zmeykovo, at least the land as we now know it, was born. While your world was being destroyed, ours was just beginning."

Theo wanted to ask what had caused the event, but he preferred not to interrupt the story. He'd been taught about meteors that had caused the Earth's ice age, but he'd never heard anything like this version of the story. Perhaps this all happened at the same time as the event that created Rabisha Lake and the Water Bull.

"A small group of humans survived in the caves," Magda continued, still in a chanting-like voice. "Surprisingly, they discovered a place that held not only hot springs, as you might expect, but also cold ones. And rivers and waterfalls also abounded there, enabling them to survive. It was those same water bodies that nourished our holy Znahar Tree."

Magda paused, as if to recollect the rest of the story. Theo sat with hands folded and eyes glued to her. He didn't dare breathe too loudly for fear he'd break the enchantment.

Drawing a deep breath, Magda resumed her tale. "Bendis claimed this land for our people, all of them, but dragons were the first to arrive, born of the molten core of the Earth. The Firebird, too, had this origin, but she arose through the Znahar Tree in fiery splendor. Other creatures arrived little by little, each created from the very land itself: the Ispolini from the mountain rocks as they jutted from the ground, the Kukeri from the elements, each taking on a different power, and the same with each being who claimed this land as their own. The Samodivi were a special mix of every part of the land: water, air, fire, earth, and spirit, all combining to make the glorious beings that we are."

Theo thought about Zima's death and how Zmey had said the Kuker's spirit returned from where it had come. Diva had always said they were beings of nature. Now, Theo understood it better. Although he still grieved the loss of his friend, Theo felt a little more comforted. The land that had birthed the Kuker had called him back to her embrace.

Magda took slow, steady breaths. "Hala, Zmey and Lamia's mother, became the first protector of the Znahar Tree. She was both priestess and queen of the land. Over time, however, possessing the sacred privilege consumed her, and her heart hardened against the people. She wanted more and more power."

Theo recalled stories he'd already heard about Hala. How she had annihilated the Ispolini, the giants, and how later Lamia had killed her mother and used her dragon scales to cover her book of secrets, *Lamia's Bible*. He'd never realized there had been a good side to Hala. No one had spoken about it.

"But before Hala became corrupted, she served the sacred tree and Bendis well," Magda continued. "As the tree thrived, it sucked the poison from the human world, and those people living beneath the mountain were able to return aboveground. But their bodies had changed while deprived of sunlight."

Again, Magda paused as if daring him to interrupt. As he fidgeted next to her, a small smile crept over her lips, and her eyes held a twinkle Theo had never seen. He hoped she wasn't making this all up to entertain him. He wanted his two worlds to have a common connection. It would make his being a part of both more meaningful.

Magda started again. "The humans' bones had become flexible and durable like plastic. In order to travel within their underground world, they made artificial wings, because their legs wouldn't support them. When they eventually exited their subterranean world, the sunlight caused their skin to crack and flake like snakes, making their bodies look as if they bore dragon scales."

Magda stopped talking for so long that Theo didn't know whether she'd finished or not. He opened his mouth to ask a question, but Magda held up her hand to stop him.

"You're wondering what happened to them next, aren't you?" she asked.

He nodded.

"They felt the pull of the Znahar Tree," Magda said. "They came to Zmeykovo to receive its healing power. Many remained, but a lot returned to the human world. Whatever path they chose, they all became full-blooded dragons, able to change at will."

Finally, Theo spoke. "Are there any of them still around?"

Magda shook her head. "Full-blooded dragons are rare these days. Over time, couples discovered they couldn't produce offspring together, so they started marrying humans. Both male and female dragons practiced this custom."

Theo nodded. "Yah, I'm familiar with the last part. We have a lot of rituals to protect girls from being kidnapped by dragons. I used to think it was all bunk, but after Lamia snatched Nia out of my hands, well … I know better now."

"I guess your rituals aren't effective." Magda smirked.

Theo crossed his arms over his chest. "If Nia had gone to the ceremony the way she was supposed to, I'm sure she would have been protected."

"Right." Skepticism coated Magda's word.

"Do dragons only marry humans these days?" Theo imagined what kind of offspring Kikimora would have if she had married a dragon. An enormous flying chicken with a snake tail. He snickered.

"What's so funny about dragons marrying humans?" Magda scowled. "Your father was supposed to marry a human. Lamia had even found one for him."

"What?" All those children Lamia had stolen over the years. Were they brought here as wives for dragon lords? "But … but he loved my mother."

"Yes, and he ruined everything because of that," Magda snapped at him. "Anyway, I thought you wanted to learn about Colobari, not dragon history?"

"I do, but dragon history has been fascinating, too. Thank you for sharing it with me." Theo tucked away the things Magda had told him. He'd search some more for books about Zmeykovo's history later. "So, if Colobar means 'little dragon,' is that why you weren't accepted?"

Magda gritted her teeth. "No, that was an ancient rule that a Colobar had to have dragon blood. I don't have much else I can tell you about the Colobari except that they've always been indispensable to the army, who called them 'the great priests.' In your human world, you'd probably call them magicians, wizards, or seers since they do fortune-telling or magical rites and incantations, and they predict when it will be a favorable time to go to battle."

"Do you have a lot of battles in Zmeykovo?"

"We're at war now with Zlo, in case you've forgotten." Magda clenched and unclenched her fists.

"Sorry. Anything else about them?" Theo stayed quiet so she could finish. He hadn't meant to irritate her so much.

"One thing." Magda leaned closer and whispered, "Colobari can *smell* emotions and thoughts, your very soul, in fact, if you don't know how to mask it. And only another Colobar has the ability to hide their scent. They can even smell and see traces of emotions you've left behind, so there's no hiding from them. The aromas are like delicate glowing cobwebs and leave a shiny trail."

Theo's heart sped up, feeling like Magda's words were a prologue to a horror scene.

"And they better not catch you here. They're getting ready to leave your father's room." Magda jumped up from the bench and sprinted away.

Theo stifled a scream and took off in the direction Magda had left. She was nowhere in sight, so he hid in an alcove outside of Zmey's room.

He froze. He could now clearly discern the words the men were saying inside.

They indeed were ending their meeting with Zmey. One of them said, "So, we're all agreed this is our plan?" One by one, voices answered, "Yes." Even Zmey uttered what sounded like a reluctant affirmation of whatever plan they had made.

It wasn't so much hearing the men that set Theo's emotions raging. He was certain this was where Magda had been standing when Theo had been talking with Zmey earlier in the day. Had she been listening to them? Or had she just happened to walk by at the moment Zmey had become feverish?

Theo hadn't wanted to spy on the men, but he made up his mind to follow them to see if he could find out what it was Zmey didn't want to do.

The door opened, and three men left the room. They were dressed in white robes, with their heads covered with hoods like monks. They even had perfected the slow-paced, gliding walk of monks. Two of the men went down a hallway that led to the castle entrance, but the third man scuttled down another corridor.

That's the one to follow, Theo thought. He crept after the man, hoping that he really couldn't smell Theo's intent.

The Colobar made his way to the small ballroom, where Theo had been staring at the statue of the two dragons earlier. The man passed by the statue without a glance and went to the fireplace. Theo hadn't paid much attention to it before because the statue had consumed his interest. Now, he looked more closely.

The fireplace was a design he hadn't seen before. Smooth black fieldstone made up the façade, but he was more intrigued by the three openings, one facing straight on, while the other two slanted to either side at about a sixty-degree angle. The opening of each was six-sided. The chimney stack that rose from it had the same basic shape as the face, with three separate panels. On each of them, a white marble panel, with what he thought were ancient Thracian symbols, rose to the ceiling. Numerous black obsidian dragon figures lined the length of the mantle. The entire wall behind the fireplace was covered with stones shaped like golden scales.

The Colobar reached for the third dragon figure from the left and pushed it toward the wall. A creaking began, and the scales parted to open the wall, revealing a hidden passageway. The Colobar slipped through the opening, and Theo hurried after him before it closed.

He followed the Colobar through twisting tunnels until he realized he'd never be able to find his way back on his own. What choice did he have now, though? Maybe the man would lead Theo somewhere familiar. After a while, the man disappeared, and a bright light flared up ahead. Theo scrambled along the passageway to where the light shone. He peeked around the corner and gasped.

He was in Zmey's treasure room, where they had brought Baba Yaga in what seemed ages ago for her "reward" for helping get rid of Sitara's curse. What did the Colobar want here? Theo doubted the man intended to rob Zmey. It must have been part of the plan they'd all agreed upon, but what was it? Theo now wished he had used his dragon hearing to learn what they were up to. He didn't want to spy on his father, but he was afraid something bad was going to happen.

Where is the Colobar? Theo examined the room, but found no one there. *How did he escape? When I searched the room the first time, I didn't find another exit.*

He went to the far end of the room where he'd heard a noise before and ran his hands all along the wall, but still no hidden door opened. *The man couldn't have just disappeared, could he?* Or maybe he could, if he was a magician.

Diva had talked about secrets before. Did she know about the passageway from the ballroom? Had she discovered it by accident or was it part of her plan when she took over the kingdom?

Theo shook his head. *I can't keep accusing Diva of betraying me without proof. I don't really believe that she would do that.*

Scratching and muted voices came from the other side of the wall again.

I have to find out who's there.

Theo went to leave the treasure room. Under the torch, he found a piece of parchment that hadn't been there when he'd entered. Had the Colobar lost it? Theo picked it up and read the words: *Follow your fate, Young Dragon Prince, and you will succeed.*

He shivered. The message was for him. The Colobar had seen Theo in the room and was aware he'd been following the man. Theo placed a hand to his head. What fate had the Colobar seen for Theo?

"I'd much rather have a note that says 'Trust Diva' or 'Trust Magda,' and not one that says 'Follow your fate.' Why can't anyone just tell me what to do, instead of giving me riddles?"

A soft chuckle bounced around the walls of the cavernous room. As it died down, a deep voice whispered in Theo's ear, "Then how would you grow and learn, Young Dragon Prince? You must be able to determine what is the truth. Your heart will lead you."

A gold coin dropped by Theo's feet, and the voice whispered again, "Here's a clue to your other question about why I'm here … and it's not to rob your father."

A breeze stirred the air, followed by the soft chuckle again, and then all was quiet.

Theo picked up the coin. *Payment for services to my father perhaps?*

The scratching and low voices from another room came again. *I can't worry about my fate or why the Colobar was in the treasure room. I have to find out who else is down here.*

Theo put out the torch and exited the treasure room. Using his dragon hearing to amplify the voices, he traveled through more passageways until he came to a set of ornate wooden doors. He inched the doors open, and stepped back at what he saw.

He'd come face-to-face once more with Sly—who stood in a room filled with books.

Chapter 4
More Secrets Unearthed

BOOKS LAY SCATTERED everywhere Theo looked. A massive library stood in front of him. Built-in bookshelves covered every wall from floor to ceiling. More books were piled high around the room, some looking as if they were ready to topple. In one corner, a ladder on wheels was pushed up tight to the shelves. Next to it, part of the bookshelf was opened like a door, which led to another room that appeared to contain even more books.

Theo gazed around once more at the massive library, and then finally said, "Sly, what are you doing here? And … and … how did you get here?"

Sly screamed, "Oh oh oh. My King, you can't be here!" He scrambled around the room, knocking over books while muttering, "So much danger. Sly didn't break his promises."

"Please stop, Sly!" Theo shouted. "I know you didn't break your promises. You're very good about not breaking promises.

You're not going to get into trouble. Will you please stop running around and come back here to talk with me?"

Sly stopped scampering, but stayed where he was. Theo wiggled his fingers for the Vodnik to come closer. "Please, Sly?"

With his head lowered and still muttering to himself, "So much danger. Sly in so much trouble," Sly hopped over.

"Sly," Theo crouched to the Vodnik's level. "I'm going to ask you questions. I'm not trying to make you break promises, but, I mean, wow, it's so unexpected to see you here, to find this amazing place. What can you tell me about it that won't break your promises?"

The trembling Vodnik looked up and said, "Lots of books here."

Theo slapped his head and laughed. "I can see that. But I heard you talking with someone earlier. Can you tell me who else is here?"

"Oh no no no. Sly not break promises."

This is getting me nowhere, Theo thought as he tapped his fingers against the floor. He stood and said, "I'm going to take a look—"

Squeaking and scraping like another book ladder being rolled around came from the other room. Theo ran over and peeked through the door opening before Sly could interfere or mention yet again he couldn't break promises. An elderly man had stepped onto the ladder and was arranging books. Something about him was familiar. All Theo could see was the man's back and the tuft of reddish-blond hair on top of his head.

No, it can't be, can it?

Theo called out, "Jabalaka?"

"Whaaa—?" The man twisted around, dropping books. His foot slipped, and he fell to the floor.

"It *is* you!" Theo ran into the room and helped Jabalaka to his feet. "We all thought you were dead. I saw you jump out of the window at Kaleto Fortress."

Theo recalled that fateful day. They had closed a portal and stopped Zlo from releasing demons into the human world. Instead, the demons now roamed Zmeykovo. Theo and Diva had fought off Zlo and Lamia and rescued Jabalaka from the torture room. They had almost all escaped, but Lamia had returned to the room. Jabalaka had been so terrified that, even though he was terribly weak and injured, he had somehow managed to climb on top of the throne and hurl himself out of a shattered window. He hadn't even screamed as he fell.

The once-frogman dusted off his bottom and scowled at Theo. "Well, you almost made good on that assumption, terrifying me like that. I could have broken my neck!"

"I'm sorry. Didn't you hear me shouting in the big room and know I was here?"

"Oh, oh, oh. No. I was in my bedroom." Jabalaka pointed to another room off of the smaller library room.

Theo couldn't stop tears from forming. He threw his arms around Jabalaka and squeezed as hard as he could. "I'm so happy to see you again."

"There, there, it's okay." Jabalaka patted Theo's back. "I survived."

Sniffling, Theo pulled away. "But how? You can't fly, can you? And it was a long way down. You should have been smashed on the rocks."

"No, I can't fly, but I have a friend who can."

Jabalaka explained how one of the deer from Sur's herd had taken a liking to him, and they had developed a companion bond. The deer constantly flew around the fortress, trying to find a way inside to rescue his friend. All Jabalaka had to do was whistle to his four-footed, six-winged friend, and the deer arrived straightaway.

"Of course, then I had to go into hiding and not let anyone know I was alive." Jabalaka shuddered. "I didn't want Lamia finding me again."

"How did you end up here?"

"I always knew about this place." Jabalaka waved his hand around the room. "I've copied many a book from here to keep at my place in the swamp."

"So … so … none of the books that Lamia burned are lost? They were all copies?"

Jabalaka nodded. "Exactly."

Theo whistled. "Wow! Diva will be so happy to know that. She was devastated with their loss. She thought all Zmeykovo's history was gone."

Jabalaka looked at Theo sideways. "So, I had been kidnapped, my home and books burned, and she worried about Zmeykovo's history?"

"No, no. She was worried about you, too. Fighting to get you back was something she was confident about. But you know Diva and her love of books. She was heartbroken."

"Uh-huh." Jabalaka nodded. "But you must not tell *anyone* about the library and me. Not Diva. Not your father. Not my sons. NO ONE must know I'm alive."

"How come Sly knows?"

"Ah, yes. My faithful little trainee." Jabalaka smiled and looked toward the other room.

Sly stood shaking in the doorway. "I break promises. Master will send me away now."

Jabalaka gestured toward the Vodnik. "Sly, my dear friend, come here."

Sly held his head so close to the floor as he hopped over that his beard trailed under his webbed hands and feet. He stopped and lay prone by Jabalaka's feet.

Jabalaka sat on the floor and lifted the Vodnik's head. "Sly, my dear friend, you did not break your promises. Theo found his own way here. I'm not going to send you away. I need you here to help me the way you have been."

Sly looked up. "Really, Master?"

"Really, my friend. You still have important tasks to help me with. I can't do it without you."

"Oh, thank you, thank you, Master. I not disappoint you." With that, Sly hopped out into the other room, where sounds of shuffling of books began.

Theo was glad that Sly was happy again, but he still wanted to know how Sly had earned the privilege of knowing Jabalaka's hiding place. Granted, the Vodnik didn't reveal the secret, but why had Jabalaka entrusted anyone with the location?

"Yes, I see the questions in your eyes," Jabalaka said. "I didn't seek out our webbed friend. He found me. You see, I used to teach him how to read here."

It now all made sense to Theo that Jabalaka was the one whose secret Sly had been protecting. The Vodnik's use of the "Oh, oh, oh" that Jabalaka often said should have given Theo a clue. But he'd thought the Keeper of Secrets had died.

"It appears that when I was kidnapped, someone told Sly that I would let him assist in building a new library." Jabalaka stared pointedly at Theo.

Theo felt his face warming and quickly said, "We said you *might* let him. Since he said you'd been teaching him to read, and he'd already helped you hide *Lamia's Bible*, it seemed a reasonable assumption for his bravery."

Jabalaka's body stiffened. "That accursed book. Glad to be rid of it. I never thanked you for killing her in the first place to end her enchantment on me."

"I'm glad it worked." Theo smiled to himself, remembering the crusty old frog creature Jabalaka had been.

"Anyway, Sly came here every day, apparently, just to look at all the books and wait for me to return." Jabalaka looked fondly into the other room, where Sly was busy putting books in order. "I'm glad he did. Since I no longer know all the secrets from that terrible book, Sly has been my eyes and ears to everything that's happening in Zmeykovo."

Theo didn't want to ask if Jabalaka knew about Zima's death. It was hard enough for Theo to deal with the loss. He didn't want to have to see Jabalaka's pain at losing a child. But Zmey had told Theo to seek out Jabalaka, so maybe he could help with Theo's problems.

He said, "So, you know Lamia's taken Zmey's ouroboros belt, and my father's dying?"

Jabalaka shivered at Theo's aunt's name. "Yes, I know what that vile creature's been up to. I may know a way for you to trick her, so you can get the belt back."

"Really?"

"Really." Jabalaka led Theo into a small room. This one held a bed, bureau, and other assorted furniture. Books littered the blankets. "When Sly told me all the things you said to him, I started searching through some ancient books to see how to take advantage of your aunt's weaknesses."

"If anyone would know them, it'd be you, since you recorded everyone's secrets."

"So true, but that's not an ability I'd wish on anyone." Sadness tinged Jabalaka's eyes. "Tell me, what do you know about the Golden Apple?"

Theo told Jabalaka everything the priestess Kosara had said. That the Znahar Tree normally only produced an apple every thousand years, but the fruit had blossomed early because of the Firebird's rebirth. She'd said it was a new cycle of life for Zmeykovo, and changes were coming. That didn't necessarily mean peace, since the Golden Apple caused discord and rioting among the deity, demons, and anyone who craved power. Whoever ate the fruit would become like the gods, and depending on their nature, could be even more formidable. Zlo had murdered the bird to force the Znahar Tree to produce the fruit, so he could take over the human world.

"Good, good." Jabalaka nodded while stroking his chin. "A key piece of information is missing, though. Only the closest direct male or female from the royal line to rule Zmeykovo can eat the apple."

"So that means Lamia or me?" Theo could feel his pulse quicken. "And since Zlo controls Lamia, that is how he plans to become ruler. Lamia would be his puppet?"

Theo thought about the different times Lamia had asked him to join forces with her against Zlo. He'd thought it was all a lie, but maybe she'd been sincere. She wanted to rule, but not under Zlo's influence.

"Exactly." Jabalaka nodded and picked up a book with a dark-red cover that was cracked and peeling. "All the problems with the gods and demons happened because they chose the royal they wanted to rule. This book"—he tapped the cover and handed the book to Theo—"chronicles all the times the Golden Apple was produced, and all the strife that ensued because of it. It'll help you understand the power of the apple and its connection with Zmeykovo. I think you'll find ways to defeat Lamia in here."

"*Lodge of Light and Lodge of Darkness*," Theo read the book's title. That was the book his father had mentioned. As Theo's dragon powers increased, he'd gained the ability to read the old language. On its cover was the same symbol on the key Zmey had shown Theo, the Celestial Turtle. As Theo leafed through the yellowed pages, he asked, "But how does this help me get my father's belt back?"

"Trickery, Theo. Lamia craves the Golden Apple. She wants power and eternity." Jabalaka tapped his temple. "Use the same deceitful tactics she would. If she thinks you have the apple, she'll try to steal it. Force her to go to a place where you maintain the advantage."

Chapter 5
Deceiving a Dragon

BACK IN THE GAZEBO, Theo read what he called the *Lodge* book. He understood some words, because his sword had awoken that ability. In various parts of the book, however, unfamiliar characters filled the yellowed pages. He tried to grasp their meaning by examining the ink illustrations, even if they were half-erased by time.

Zmeykovo had experienced a violent history, much like his own world. A lot of it was attributed to power-crazed people—for lack of a better term to call the residents of Zmeykovo—vying for the Golden Apple. As he read, an idea began brewing in his mind about how to draw Lamia to the castle, so he and his friends could overpower her.

He shivered as he laid the book on his lap. To gain a sense of tranquility after reading about so many horrors, he took a moment to marvel again at the roses. He'd ended up back in the garden after he'd left the library. Jabalaka had explained how to return to the upper rooms of the castle but advised against using the passageways that led to the small ballroom. Theo couldn't be certain that no one would be there when he returned. Instead, Jabalaka showed Theo the way Sly came and went from the library. When Theo had arrived at the end of that passageway, he'd laughed. It exited beneath the rose garden gazebo.

"Oh, did you find something interesting to read?" Diva asked, looking over his shoulder. Today, she wore a green robe, instead of her usual white one, and an ivy wreath circled her curly blond locks. "I love books, but I've already read all the ones that are left here."

Theo slammed the book shut and slid it under his thigh, out of Diva's view. "No, just some fantasy novel."

Pavel strolled down the path. "So this is where you've been hiding all day, man. I've been looking all over for you."

Theo shrugged. "I sat with my father for a while."

It tore Theo apart not being able to tell his friends everything that had happened. He looked at Diva, searching for hints that she was uneasy in his presence, that she had something to hide. But the Samodiva remained serene, her usual demeanor.

Pavel, on the other hand, still had dark circles under his eyes. He tried to hide the pain, the guilt he felt about Zima's death, but Theo knew his friend well enough to understand it was tearing Pavel apart. Since that day, he hadn't even used any of his favorite exclamations like "doggie doo" or "bat guano." Pavel had had to grow up quickly. *And so have I,* Theo thought. Too bad growing up meant keeping secrets from friends.

"How's your father doing? Any better?" Diva sat next to Theo and laid her hand on his shoulder.

He cringed, still not sure of her motives.

Diva gave him a questioning lock. She straightened her ivy crown and blew curls out of her face as if to say that was why she removed her hand that had meant to comfort him.

"Not good." Theo avoided looking at Diva and hurried to cover his unease. "Zmey got feverish, and I had to scream for Magda."

"Man, that rots," Pavel said as he leaned against a railing. "I wish we could do something to help him."

"Maybe you can, all of us." He couldn't do this without his friends, whether he fully trusted them or not. His grandmother often said, "A good team can lift a mountain" and "Good friends can do anything." Theo's plan might be a way to see if Diva and Pavel both really were true friends. "I've been thinking about how I can get my father's ouroboros belt back."

Pavel slid onto the bench on the opposite side. "That'd be great. It's as dull as heck here. I mean, my room's great and all, three times bigger than my house in Selo. It's got all kinds of stuff Nia would love: golden candlesticks, a crystal chandelier, a huge fireplace, and armchairs that look like they belong in the Versailles palace. But I want to *do* something. I need an adventure."

Theo thought that Pavel's real reason for an adventure was to get his mind off of the last battle they'd fought against Lamia and her horde. The image of the spear piercing Zima's back when he jumped in front of Pavel kept playing in Theo's mind. The horror of it likely would be forever imprinted on Pavel's mind as well. But still, would Pavel be ready for another encounter with Lamia so soon? Theo's only way of finding out would be to tell them what he was planning.

"You might change your mind after I tell you what I'm thinking."

"Maybe, but you know I'll stick by you," Pavel said. "We've been friends forever. We always do crazy stuff with each other—especially here."

"And you can count me in, too," Diva added.

Theo took a deep breath, hoping that was true. He didn't know what Magda's plan was to reveal Diva's supposed deception, but he prayed his aunt was wrong.

"I want to lure Lamia here and—"

"What?" Pavel jumped up. "I know I just said we did crazy things, but that's *super*-crazy!"

"Wait, hear me out." Theo made a patting motion for Pavel to sit back on the bench. "What is it that Lamia wants most?"

"She wants you dead, that's what." Pavel perched on the edge of the seat as if ready to flee at a moment's notice.

"But she wasn't going to kill me. She—"

"No, just torture you." Pavel scowled. "In the meantime, she doesn't care how many of the rest of us she kills."

"But what's her motivation for doing everything she's done?"

Diva said in a soft voice, "She wants power and immortality."

Theo's stomach cramped. He wanted to ask if that was what Diva wanted, too, but he kept his words to himself. "Right," he finally said. "And the way she can get that is with …?"

"Gold and wealth go along with power." Pavel shrugged. "Just look at Baba Yaga. She always wants more gold. I don't know how that would give Lamia immortality, though. Besides, Lamia could have gotten her fill of anything here in the castle after she and Zlo captured Zmey."

"No, she has gold and treasures," answered Theo. "The only thing that can seduce Lamia out of her lair to come here is—"

"The Golden Apple," Diva finished. "So she and Zlo can control the world."

"And I've discovered that only the heir to Zmeykovo can pick the apple." Theo slid the book farther under his leg. That was one piece of information he'd discovered in the *Lodge* book. That had to be the reason Lamia hadn't killed Theo when she'd had the opportunity. Only he could pick the apple, not her.

"But the apple hasn't ripened yet, has it?" Pavel asked. "And, even if it did, how does that help get your father's belt back from your crazy aunt?"

"That's what I asked, um, was thinking about." Theo quickly corrected himself. He'd almost mentioned Jabalaka. He hoped neither of his friends picked up on his slip of the tongue. Maybe they'd think he was going to say he asked himself. Sly was better than Theo at not "breaking promises," as the Vodnik called it.

"I think I know what you're planning," Diva said.

"Feel free to explain it to Pavel, then. He's more likely to listen to you than to me."

Pavel's face turned red. "Hey, that's not true."

"Theo's idea is to pretend we have the apple, use it as bait. I think he's even planning on making a fake one." She turned to look at Theo, and he nodded. "If we can lure Lamia inside the castle grounds and away from the Knights of Darkness, Radan, and Lamia's hoard of Harpies and other servants who surround her, we'll have a better chance of defeating her. One against many."

"Okaaaay, but how are you going to make a decoy?"

"With this." Theo dug out the golden coin from the Colobar and flipped it in the air. The man must have planned this all along.

Maybe his vision had been of Theo making a golden apple. "Did you forget my father has a cavern full of gold?"

"A gold coin isn't an apple, though. Do you have a magic spell to change it?" Pavel opened his eyes wide. "You're not going to ask Baba Yaga to do that, are you? Tricks are her specialty."

Theo shook his head. "No, the witch always wants something in return. We can't rely on her, even though my father says she's trustworthy. She's double-crossed us too many times. I have a better idea. Who in Zmeykovo can work miracles with any kind of metal?"

Pavel scrunched up his face, thinking. "Oh, I get it. Sitara. Once we have the decoy Golden Apple, what's your plan to let Lamia know about it?"

Theo shrugged. "I've been trying to figure that out. She has spies everywhere, so maybe she'll just learn about it."

"That's not good enough." Pavel got up and paced the gazebo. "We need a plan and a backup plan. Even a plan C and D would be good. Lamia's not just going to walk in here and hand over the belt if you say, 'Please.'"

Diva nodded. "I agree. It's best to be prepared for the worst outcome."

Theo wanted to avoid a fight if possible. A couple of times already, Lamia had tried to convince him to join forces with her. Did she really want that? Was her goal truly to defeat Zlo? Maybe Zmey's belt gave her enough power that she could break away from her master. But wouldn't it be better for her to return the belt to Zmey? Then the two of them could fight Zlo together. Plus, she'd have the backing of everyone who supported Zmey. Unfortunately, all Theo had found in the *Lodge* book were battle strategies, not any method of conducting a diplomatic conversation with the enemy.

But he agreed that his friends were right. They needed to prepare for anything. "Worst case would be Lamia wouldn't come alone."

Diva added, "She might even attempt to destroy any support we could gather. Anyone living nearby would be a target."

"Then we'll need a way to protect the villagers." Theo couldn't let innocent people die. He'd seen how much the people loved Zmey. They'd all come out to cheer him when he'd returned to the castle.

"The easiest way would be to bring them into the castle." Pavel's eyes darkened. "And, I'd like to put Lamia in a cage when she comes. That's the only place a vicious animal like her belongs."

"So would I." Theo laughed, but Pavel's face remained serious.

"I wasn't joking. I was thinking we could put the Golden Apple on that pedestal on the terrace over there." Pavel pointed to where the golden roses Zunitza had planted encircled a marble pedestal. "We could secure a metal net and cage on the bottom of the balcony above it. Then when Lamia grabs the apple, first drop the net onto her so she can't move. Then drop the cage and drive wedges from it into the net to doubly hold her tight."

"Actually, that sounds like a good idea. Thanks, Pavel."

"Maybe we can get Baba Yaga to enchant—"

"No!" Theo held his hand out to stop Pavel from saying more. "I already said I don't want her help."

"You may have to get her involved." Diva's soft voice made both Theo and Pavel look her way. "We still haven't talked about a way to make sure Lamia knows we have the apple."

"But do we really have to involve the witch?" Theo's stomach ached with the thought. Couldn't he manage even one critical action without involving Baba Yaga? It felt as if they were always begging some favor from her.

"Who else then?" She replied. "Someone has to leak the information to Lamia without raising suspicion."

"Diva's right," Pavel said. "Baba Yaga has already shown she makes deals with both Lamia and us. I can't think of anyone else we could get that Lamia might believe."

"Besides," Diva added, "Baba Yaga is resourceful, and it's easy to buy her services."

Theo hated the fact that Diva was right. The conniving witch was the only one who played both sides of the fence. They'd have to involve her—again. Only this time, he wasn't going to put up with any of her nonsense.

"All right. She's the perfect one for the role, maybe the only one." Theo stood and tucked the book beneath his arm. "We'll plan on asking Baba Yaga unless we can think of something better after Sitara makes the apple. Let's get ready and grab whatever else we might need before we call the deer. It's time to pay the blacksmith a visit."

Chapter 6
A Golden Decoy

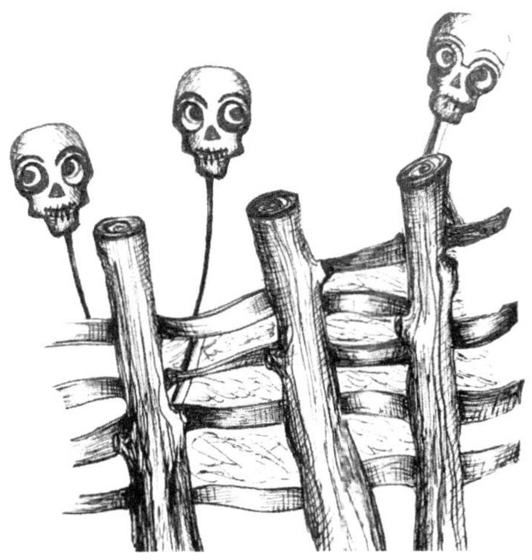

SITARA'S LAUGHTER RANG throughout the smithy. It wasn't a happy sound, but more maniacal, as if the man had been asked to do the impossible. His sandy-haired apprentice almost dropped the awl he was using to ignite the flames in the forge, as if the boy was more used to scolding words coming from his master.

"What's so funny?" Theo stood with his legs apart and hands clenched at his side. "My father's life is at stake!"

Granted, the blacksmith wasn't under any obligation to help Theo, even though he and his friends had been instrumental in restoring the man's humanity. Sitara had already gone above and beyond repaying that debt when he'd provided them weapons and embellishments to defeat the Water Bull. But Theo thought Sitara would be more than eager to help them again. Because, really, it was a big deal that the blacksmith no longer suffered the curse of being a Vurkolak, that anger-filled werewolf-like creature that preyed on any living being that crossed his path.

"Forgive me." Sitara shook his head as if trying to clear out cobwebs. "It's been a crazy day, and having you ask me to make a fake Golden Apple was the last thing I expected. I'll gladly help you."

Theo unclenched his fists and slowly let out his breath. He handed Sitara the gold coin from the Colobar.

"I can make the most beautiful, elegant, shiny Golden Apple, but not with one coin." Sitara shook his head. "I'd need at least a dozen just to coat the outside."

"I … uh …" Theo's head spun.

He felt so stupid for having misread the Colobar's intent. Theo had thought the one coin the Colobar had left would be sufficient for the job. Of course, the man wouldn't have dumped a handful at Theo's feet. The priest would have expected Theo to use his brain and get more, once he figured out what the coin was for.

"I don't have any more gold on me."

"What about Lucky's golden horns," Pavel said. "Do you still have them, Sitara? Recycle and reuse."

"I do indeed." Sitara called to his apprentice, "Go downstairs and bring up the golden horns."

The boy lowered his head in acknowledgment and scurried to the back of the room. His hurried footsteps grew fainter as he reached the lower level. Moments later, he rushed back, out of breath, and handed Sitara the two golden objects that had covered the bull's horns.

Sitara hammered the horns, and then cut off the iron tips with a steel blade. "You're fortunate I have a mold already made. I have several of these, in fact. They're popular during the wedding season." Sitara chuckled as he set down his tools and removed a ceramic crucible and an apple mold from a shelf. To his apprentice, he said, "Keep an eye on the shop while I craft this golden apple."

The boy nodded and went back to his tasks.

"I'll return when the apple's ready." Sitara walked toward the back where his apprentice had gone before.

Pavel followed closely behind. "May I watch?"

Sitara stopped, and Pavel plowed into the blacksmith. "Uh, no. Not this time. If you decide you want to learn how to be a smithy, I can take you on as a second apprentice another day."

Pavel glanced at the sandy-haired youth. Sweat had caused soot-covered trails to streak down his face. Pavel shook his head. "I'll pass."

Theo was glad not to have to return to the lower workshop, which Sitara used to forge items made from precious metals and gems. The last time Theo had been down there, he and Pavel had encountered Sitara in his Vurkolak form. The blacksmith had chained himself in a carved-out area below the kiln to prevent himself from harming anyone. Theo still recalled Sitara's bloody fangs and sharp claws. But more than that, the hatred in Sitara's eyes had chilled Theo. He thought about all the other events that had happened since that day. So much in only a little more than a week!

"Earth to Theo!" Pavel tapped Theo on the shoulder and waved the apple in front of his face "Where'd you go, man? You haven't heard a thing any of us have said to you for a couple of hours. Sitara has the apple ready."

Theo blinked and took the golden decoy. "Amazing! It looks so real." The apple was a perfect replica, including the stem and all the ridges. "You truly are a master, Sitara."

"There's one thing I can't reproduce." Sitara placed the mold back onto the shelf. "The apple's magic."

"That's okay," Theo said. "We don't want it to have any real power."

"You don't understand." Sitara came closer. "Lamia won't be fooled by this one, even if it looks exactly like the real Golden Apple. She'll be able to sense that your fake version lacks magic. You need an enchantment."

"Good to know." Theo tossed the apple into the air, acting as if that was no big deal. "We were on our way to visit Baba Yaga next. I'm sure she'll help us."

When they arrived at the meadow outside of Vida Village, where they had left their flying companions, Theo laid his head against his deer.

"Now what are we going to do?" He spoke the words out loud for Diva and Pavel, but let Shar read his thoughts about what had transpired in the smithy, hoping the deer would have a suggestion.

"*You'll find a solution,*" Shar thought back. "*I believe in you.*"

Pavel looked over from where he fed flower buds to Whirl. "What do you mean? We'll ask Baba Yaga to enchant the apple. Simple as that."

"How is that simple?" Theo combed his fingers along Shar's side to release built-up frustration. "We can't tell Baba Yaga we have a fake apple that needs an enchantment. We were going to tell her we had the *real* Golden Apple. If we ask her for an enchantment for a fake one, she'll know something's going on."

"Is there someone else we can ask?" Pavel asked.

"Kikimora?" Theo wasn't sure the chicken lady had that kind of power, but it might be worth trying.

"No!" Pavel shouted. "I told you before I would never go back there. Not after she tried to drag me into the swamp, to do who knows what."

"What about Magda?" His aunt was the best healer. She might be able to enchant an apple.

Diva shook her head. "I don't trust her. My sisters must have had a good reason for exiling your aunt from the Samodivi community. Magda might be keeping your father alive, but Sava and Ula are still keeping a close eye on your aunt for any treachery."

"But I think she's changed."

"Diva said no." Pavel now stood by their Samodiva friend's side. "I say we each get to veto one suggestion. So, no Kikimora and no Magda. If you say no to Baba Yaga, then we probably don't have anyone else who can do the enchantment."

Theo sighed. What had Zmey said earlier, that he put the needs of his people before his own? Theo had promised his father to do the same.

"Okay, Baba Yaga it is." Theo reluctantly agreed. "But you know how two-faced she is. I'm not even sure she'll be willing to help us again."

"Trust me. She will," Diva said. "The witch will be curious about what we want."

"But how are we going to prevent her from telling Lamia our true plan?"

Diva's eyes twinkled. "I have an idea. Leave it with me."

His Samodiva friend was always so certain about everything. Theo couldn't recall a time when Diva's ideas had failed them—unlike Theo's own plans that frequently went afoul. Maybe since

Diva lived according to the rule of nature and hadn't had to live with all the rules and regulations of the human world, she could discern what was the right way to accomplish something. Whatever it was, she was always sound in her judgment.

They all climbed onto their deer in silence. As the trio flew over the Forest of Whispering Bells, the chimes below announced their impending arrival. Baba Yaga's so-called "doorbell" was working again. The witch would be certain to meet them in the meadow where her hut on chicken legs resided.

The old witch leaned against the gate of her skull fence as they landed. She fiddled with the bone finger that made up the latch, flipping it up and down.

"Well, well, if it ain't my pesky beggars." She slammed the latch down, splintering the finger. "What do you expect me to do *this* time?"

Diva motioned for Theo and Pavel to stay where they were. She smiled and strode toward the gate. "We're looking for an enchantment."

"You Samodivi already have the power to enchant." Baba Yaga scoffed. "Can't you use your charms on the human boy to make him love you?"

"What?" Pavel spluttered as his face turned red. "That's what you wanted to ask Baba Yaga?"

Diva ignored him and replied to the witch, "A different kind of enchantment, one that can hide an object's magic. But we'll also need it to be able to restore it, too."

Baba Yaga scratched her chin, pulling at a scraggly hair. "That's a dangerous one. You're not planning on using this against me, are you?" She glared at Theo as she spoke.

Diva's curls danced over her forehead as she shook her head. "No, it's not a weapon to hurt you."

Baba Yaga smudged in dirt as she scratched at her earlobe. Finally, she spoke. "Well, I ain't gonna just give you that kind of enchantment without knowing what it's for! Speak up, Samodiva."

Diva leaned closer. "We have the Golden Apple, and we need to hide it from Lamia."

"He he, ho ho. Put one over on that beast." The witch hopped around and stepped on Kotka, who had crept up from behind to wrap herself around Baba Yaga's legs.

"Mrawl!" The cat flapped its purple wings and flew around the hut.

"Oh, Kotka, Kotka, come back! I'll give you a nice treat." Baba Yaga ran after the cat and scurried up the steps. "Well, come on, Samodiva, if you want that enchantment."

Diva opened the gate and held it for Theo and Pavel.

"No, not them," Baba Yaga yelled. "I don't want the dragon boy or the human boy in here."

Pavel pouted. "Theo I can understand, but what did I do?"

"Doesn't matter." The witch shook her head. "I only want the Samodiva. We have things to discuss."

While Diva went inside, Pavel walked over to pat and feed Whirl, who, along with the other deer, had invaded Baba Yaga's herb garden. The witch was going to be annoyed and probably blame it on Theo. He sighed. The deer had their own minds. He couldn't do anything about it.

He felt déjà vu. Another one of his friends was conversing with the witch while he sat outside, banned from the hut. The last time, Pavel had braved being alone with the witch so she would cure him of a curse Zima had inadvertently placed on Pavel. Although Theo didn't worry that Baba Yaga would harm Diva, the witch's statement that they had things to "discuss" bothered him. Magda's warning about Diva surfaced again, and Theo couldn't help but think that his friend was plotting against him.

He wanted to burst into the hut to tell the witch this was the most important task they'd asked her to do. His father was dying. Theo rehearsed the words he would say. "My father claims you're trustworthy. I hope he's right, because if Zmey dies, I'll become ruler. If you trick us again, I won't think kindly of you the way he does." Words he knew he'd never say. He couldn't confront anyone. Not Baba Yaga. Not Diva. Right at this moment, speaking at all would make the ache in his stomach surface, and he'd look like the coward he felt.

The hut door flew open with a bang, drawing Theo out of his melancholy mood.

Baba Yaga wore a huge grin. "And you'll remind your sisters not to forget about my new Chutura?"

"Yes, I've already explained they'll give you a new one as soon as we get Zmeykovo back to normal." Diva waved goodbye while holding a vial with a purple liquid in her other hand.

Theo got up from the ground and wiped dirt from his pants. "Well, what do we owe the witch this time?"

"I already took care of it." Diva placed the vial into her pouch. "There are herbs she wants that only grow in the Samodivi forest. I'll have someone bring them to her when they have a chance."

"Anything else?" Theo tried to peer into Diva's soul. "What did she want to discuss?"

Diva cocked her head to the side and shrugged. "Just how to make the enchantment if we needed more."

"That's it? And all she wanted was herbs?"

Diva nodded. "They're special ones that only Samodivi can give her. Besides, she said it was a favor for Zmey, her old friend and protector."

"O-okay."

"Hey, guys!" Pavel climbed onto Whirl. "Let's go. I'm starving."

Theo gave Pavel a thumbs-up and walked toward Shar. "I guess that was so much easier than our original plan. Do you think the witch will go running off to blabber to Lamia that we have the Golden Apple, hoping she'll get another reward?"

"Absolutely." Diva smiled, sending chills spiraling through Theo.

Chapter 7
An Urgent Message

FROM THE CASTLE, Theo gazed at the puffs of black smoke from the hut on chicken legs that peppered the sky all the way to Kaleto Fortress. Baba Yaga had flown straight to Lamia as they'd expected. The witch's old mortar, her "Chutura," was most certainly on its last legs. It was no wonder she kept asking when the Samodivi would deliver the one they had promised her. That seemed like ages ago.

He paced the rose garden, where he had returned after he, Pavel, and Diva had landed. Theo's heart ached, not knowing if he could trust Diva or not. Surely, she hadn't told Baba Yaga their real plan, had she?

Either way, they'd likely have "guests" soon. He had to prepare for Lamia's arrival. Get nets and a cage from the Kukeri. Arm everyone with weapons. Find hiding spots. Enchant and put the fake apple—

"Theo! There you are." Magda's voice rang out. "Have you been here the entire time I left you?"

Theo ran toward her. "What's the matter? Did something happen to my father?"

"No, no, nothing like that." She wiped stray hairs from her face, flushed from running. "You have visitors."

"Who?" he asked out loud while thinking, *Surely Lamia hasn't arrived already and knocked at the front gate.*

"Messengers from Kosara."

Magda led Theo through a part of the castle he had yet to explore. His aunt's figure slithered down the passageway with silent steps. He passed a door with the symbol of the Celestial Turtle carved into the panes. The same symbol on the key his father wore on a chain around his neck. Theo tried the door, but it was locked. His fingers tingled where the tips touched the wooden frame.

Is magic keeping people out? I wonder what's in there.

"Hurry up, Theo," Magda hissed from down the passageway. "The messengers are waiting. There's no time to waste."

"I'm coming." Theo hastened his steps to keep up.

Magda stopped at a heavy mahogany door decorated with bas-reliefs of dragons sitting on thrones. When Theo followed his aunt inside, a calming sensation came over him. This was a place a ruler went to escape from tasks and worries. Ambient light cast a gentle aura throughout the room, and the smell of old books filled the air. The room felt as if it was welcoming him home.

The place looked like a study. An enormous mahogany desk was situated in front of arched stained-glass windows, depicting battle scenes with dragons. Two white-marble statues stood on either side of the desk. Built-in shelves lining the walls held scant books. Those that were displayed had engraved spines. Theo would tell Diva about it later. Perhaps these were some of the books she thought were lost forever in the fire that ravaged Jabalaka's home.

The main thing that caught his eye, though, was a large gilt-framed painting of Zunitza. His mother was decked out in royal finery. A delicate crown like one he'd never seen before graced her hair. It was more like an ancient artifact. Instead of having upward pointing spikes, thin, golden leaves twisted around a headband. Others hung along delicate golden chains that dangled to shoulder length. Chips of precious gems were nestled among the golden leaves. Emeralds. Sapphires. Diamonds. The shimmering jewels reflected the color of nature. The painter had caught the light shining on them in a dazzling display of colors. The overall effect was like experiencing the wonders of a magical forest.

Magda hissed in his ear, "Theo, don't be rude. Welcome your guests."

He looked around the room. "Where are they?"

Magda gave him a strange look. "Right in front of you."

Heat rose to Theo's neck and cheeks. He'd barely glanced at what he'd thought were statues. The messengers' faces were shadowed by the hooded robes they wore, with only a scant amount of hair peeking out. Each man wore a necklace with the Celestial Turtle symbol.

One of the messengers moved closer and spoke in a soft voice, "Greetings, Young Dragon Prince. We are ambassadors sent from our most-honored priestess, Kosara, the guardian of the sacred Znahar Tree."

Theo twitched. "Oh, greetings …" He wasn't sure how to address the man, so he opted for "sir ambassador."

"We bring you a private missive and request your response." The man removed from the folds of his robe a mother-of-pearl box inlaid with a tree of life and handed it to Theo.

Magda reached for it, but Theo placed his hand on her arm, stopping her.

"Don't you need me to read it?" she asked quietly.

"No, he said it's private." Theo nodded toward the door. "Thank you for bringing me here, but could you please look after my father now? I'll find my way back okay."

Magda's face tightened, and she gave Theo a curt nod. When the door closed behind him, Theo opened the box and removed a rolled parchment. A wax seal with the Celestial Turtle symbol had been pressed to keep the letter closed. Theo broke the seal and read Kosara's message:

Dearest Young Dragon Prince, I know the title likely makes you uncomfortable, but this is our custom. This is a special message for the Dragon Palace. The Golden Apple has ripened. We must conduct a harvesting ceremony immediately. My ambassadors will escort you and Zmey to the Znahar Tree. Please allow them to perform their duties according to tradition.

Theo rolled up the parchment and placed it back into the box. The letter said to bring Zmey. Kosara would have to understand Theo wasn't going to do that. To the ambassadors, he said, "I'm sorry that my father is not here to welcome you. I must also let you know he is too unwell to participate in the ceremony."

The men bowed their heads. "As you wish."

"Kosara said the ceremony must be done immediately," Theo said. "Do I have time to get my friends? They can come, too, can't they?" Theo really needed to talk with Diva and Pavel. This turn of events was complicating the plans they had for capturing Lamia this evening.

"Whatever the Young Dragon Prince requires." The men bowed again. "We also have this for your highness to wear." The second man pulled another box from within his robe and handed it to Theo.

What I require, Theo thought, *is not to be treated like royalty. I'm just a boy, not ready to be a ruler*. Out loud, he said as he took the box, "Thank you. I'll be ready as soon as I can, so I don't keep Kosara waiting."

"We will escort you to the Znakar Tree," the first messenger said. "Wait for us by the front gate."

When Theo left the room, a dark shadow flickered along the wall in the torch light. He wanted to follow it, but changed his mind. *It's just a shadow, and I don't have time to waste.*

He hurried back the way he came and went to Pavel's room first. Theo wanted to see what his friends thought about how the new event would affect their plans. The door to Pavel's room was open, and voices came from within. Diva sat cross-legged on Pavel's bed next to him, both looking at a diagram on the covers.

"Hey, guys," Theo said as he walked into the room. "We might have a problem."

His friends stopped talking, and Pavel folded the paper and stuffed it into his backpack that lay next to him. A glass sound clinked against metal.

"A new invention?" Theo asked.

Pavel hadn't mentioned anything about having a new idea. Theo felt his best friend slipping further away. It was hard to blame Pavel. Theo had spent most of the last few days either with his father or trying to find a way to get Zmey's belt back and hadn't been there to help Pavel through his own grief at Zima's loss.

Pavel shrugged. "So, what's the problem?"

Theo told them about Kosara's request to harvest the apple. "Now we're not going to have time to set up our trap for Lamia. We haven't even had a chance to ask the Kukeri to help us."

"We'll be fine." Diva stood and stretched. "This will actually be better."

"How do you figure?" Theo asked.

"I know you don't trust Baba Yaga," Diva replied. "So, now it doesn't matter what the witch told Lamia. News will get back to her that we have the real Golden Apple. It's a good bet Lamia will come to get it. Even if we don't have the cage set up, we can fight her."

"Aw, man." Pavel snapped his fingers. "I wanted to see her in a cage."

"I guess we'll have to lock her behind the bars in Magura Cave, where she held my father."

Theo opened the box the second messenger had given him. Inside lay a Turkish blue robe, the color of the night sky. Gold trim had been embroidered around the neckline, sleeves, and hem. The buttons were crafted in the shape of dragon claws. Theo turned the garment around to see the back. A white dragon, with wings spread wide, soared through the air.

Pavel touched the material. "Wow, it's so soft. Put it on, Theo, Your Royal Highness."

"I'm not royal anything. I feel silly," Theo mumbled as he slid the robe over his clothing. "Okay, we need to hurry. I'll get my stuff and be back. Pack up whatever you think you'll need to pick an apple."

Theo rushed to his own room, grabbed his backpack, and made his way back to Pavel's room. Diva held her pouch and bow and arrow. A ribbon embellished the straps on her shoulder, and she'd wound an ivy belt around her waist. Theo tensed, thinking about Magda's earlier accusation.

Did Diva take my mother's belt? He really wanted to know, and maybe he'd try later to find out—without Magda's help. Now wasn't the right time to ask. They were in enough of a hurry, and bringing up the matter would only create tension between them.

"Just a little more." Pavel, red in the face, was shoving a coiled-up rope into his backpack—or attempting to. It stuck out of the top, looking like a late-riser having a bad hair day.

"What's your genius idea for bringing along a rope?" Theo laughed. "Or are you just having a wrestling match with it to show Diva how strong you are?"

"Noooo." Pavel scowled and yanked out the rope, tossing it onto his bed. "I wanted to be prepared in case Kosara doesn't have a ladder to get to the apple. But since you obviously don't want my help …"

"Sorry. It's a great idea. Thanks for thinking about me." Theo took a step closer. "But I'm sure Kosara has everything we need at the Znahar Tree. I guess we should hurry. Kosara's note said the ceremony had to be performed immediately."

"I've called Sur and the deer." Diva moved toward the door. "They'll be waiting for us by the main gate."

Sur nuzzled Diva when they left the castle. The two of them appeared to be conversing silently. The deer snorted and dug his hooves into the ground.

"Is everything okay?" Theo asked.

"Sur says we have to be on high alert if the apple's ready. He remembers the last time …" Diva trailed off. "It wasn't pretty."

Theo nodded as she spoke. He'd read about the gruesome slaughter that had happened when the apple had last ripened. "Maybe I should shift into a dragon and fly us there. It might be safer."

Sur snorted again. Theo didn't need any interpretation to understand that Sur was saying he was more powerful than any dragon.

"Okay, then. Let's get the other deer and leave."

A voice behind Theo said, "I hope you don't mind if I join you for the ceremony."

Theo spun around. Magda approached, wearing black riding breeches and a black blouse. She'd reverted to her usual dark attire. Her snake bracelets were once again visible, and her hair hung in those creepy braids.

Pavel slid closer to Diva. "Man, Theo, your aunt dresses like a black widow."

Theo rolled his eyes. He was less concerned about how Magda was dressed than he was about how she knew he was leaving to harvest the apple. He had told only Diva and Pavel. Maybe his aunt had figured out that the apple had ripened because the messengers had come to the castle.

He asked Magda, "What about Zmey? He needs constant care."

"I've asked Ula to sit with him for a while." When Theo shrugged, Magda looked toward the herd. "I need a deer, too."

Theo didn't answer right away. He looked from Magda to the deer. "I thought all Samodivi already had deer companions."

Magda sighed. "Mine died when I was a girl."

Theo's dragon senses tingled. The way Magda spoke the words sounded ominous. He didn't ask for details, not in front of his friends. His aunt had opened up to him earlier today, but she wasn't likely to do so now, with an audience. There would be time for that later—if he dared broach the topic. Right now, they had to make it to the ceremony.

"Since you've had one before, I guess you know what to do." Theo waved to the herd, and Magda took steps toward a young deer with magnificent antlers.

Sur lowered his head and dug deep grooves in the ground. The orb between his antlers glowed and swirled, flashing a dark purple.

"Diva, what's the matter with Sur?" Theo asked.

"He's not happy about Magda." She stroked his fur. "He says he can't stop it if a deer chooses her, though."

"Why, what happened?"

"He didn't give me details, only that she was responsible for the animal's death."

Snorting, the stag Magda approached stepped away. Purple danced through his orb. Theo recalled how a deer's orb would turn amber as a sign of accepting someone for a companion. The deer could sense a person's soul and intent, at least Shar had when he'd accepted Theo. Deer and person formed an eternal bond, each being able to read the other's thoughts, at least with time. The deer Magda approached obviously didn't like what it saw in her.

Magda scuffed her feet in the dirt. "Fine. I'll find someone else. It doesn't matter who."

She moved toward a small deer standing on the side of the herd. It stood still as if shocked, and Theo understood where the saying about a deer-in-the-headlights look came from. As Magda reached out to climb onto the deer, it lost its stare and darted away.

Every deer Magda approached avoided her. Theo felt bad. The pain in her heart was marring her ability to connect with another deer.

Her face flushed, she said with a growl in her voice, "I guess today's not a day for riding. I'll fly to the Znahar Tree myself." She spun in a circle and shifted into a black raven, disappearing into the cloudy sky.

"Oh, man," Pavel said, "your aunt is so strange."

Diva scowled as Magda flew away. "You shouldn't have said she could come, Theo. You can't trust her."

Funny, he thought, *she said the same about you, Diva.*

His aunt was strange, but Theo felt compassion toward her because of what she'd suffered. Everyone viewed their own life differently from what others saw. Both Diva and Magda could be right about not trusting the other—in their own minds, at least. Magda had obviously suffered at the hands of other Samodivi, and so she automatically distrusted Diva. And Diva had heard stories about Magda from her sisters and now Sur. But Diva herself had never had much direct contact with Magda, so everything she believed was second-hand.

Theo had no reason to distrust either Diva or Magda at the moment. He chided himself for even thinking Diva would betray him. She'd stood by him ever since he'd come to Zmeykovo the first time.

Theo shrugged. "Yes, she's strange, but she's family."

"So is Lamia," Pavel said. "And you wouldn't invite her. Are we going to leave now?"

"No." Theo looked around. "Kosara's messengers said to wait here for them to escort us."

Right on cue, the ambassadors stepped out of the castle. One man pointed to the sky. "Your transportation has arrived, Young Dragon Prince."

"We were going to ride ..." Theo didn't finish the thought.

The object the ambassadors pointed to had landed: a silver flying carriage, drawn by two white creatures, looking like a mix between dragon and horse.

Chapter 8
The Golden Apple

REACHING CLOSE TO six feet tall, the creatures pulling the carriage were a mass of muscles, twisting around their scaled torsos. Their manes, tails, and wings were feathery, and as soft as the blanket Theo's mother had wrapped him in the day she left him in Selo. Spikes lined both their scaled, dragon-shaped faces and their hoofed feet.

"They're magnificent." Theo ran his hands along the sparkling wing feathers. "What are they?"

"Konedrakoni," one of the messengers replied. "Our sacred god Tangra's own breed. They are the only creatures allowed to pull the Silver Chariot of the Dragon."

Pavel slipped past Theo. "And look at this carriage. It's straight out of a Disney movie."

"Pavel …" Theo started but stopped.

He hadn't really looked at what the ambassadors called the "silver chariot." He had assumed it would be like the one he had ridden in when he first arrived in Zmeykovo. Only that one was pulled by a giant three-headed snake.

Pavel was right. This new one reminded him of Cinderella's pumpkin-turned-coach—at least its shape. It was black, with silver trimming of twisting vines that wrapped around the sides and edges of the roof. Even the wheel spokes were silver. Two coachmen sat up front on a bench. At the back were a storage compartment and a silver-velvet-covered step. Handles on either side of the carriage were shaped like dragon heads and were likely for a footman or two to grasp as the vehicle sped through the air.

The most striking feature of the carriage, however, was a silver dragon sculpture atop the roof. Wings were outstretched in preparation for flight, and claws rested over the windows, as if guarding precious cargo within. The dragon's tail arched over the back, and its head hovered over the front bench like a canopy. Gemstone-encrusted eyes had a piercing stare, as if looking into Theo's soul.

He opened the doors on his side. They swung away from each other to reveal embroidered, silver-velvet-upholstered benches. Inside revealed a tight space for the three of them, when you added their weapons and backpacks. Pavel would be certain to sit next to Diva on this trip.

The overall effect of the carriage was a bit elaborate for Theo. So much pomp and circumstance to pick an apple. He wanted to object and ride the deer, but Kosara's note had said to do as the ambassadors requested.

"Well, I guess we should get in." Theo held the door for his friends. "That is, if Sur feels we'll be safe with the Konedrakoni driving us."

Sur grunted. His fireball, mostly amber, shot bits of purple sparks, to show his annoyance.

Theo, Diva, and Pavel settled down inside the carriage. Theo smiled. His prediction had been correct. Pavel sat squashed up next to Diva.

She nudged him with her elbow. "Slide over a little, so I can move my arms."

"No room. I'm wedged in myself."

"Maybe I should fly with Sur to the Znahar Tree." Diva stood.

Theo held out his hand to stop her. "No, please, let's all ride there together. I want my friends with me."

Diva grunted but squashed herself back into place. "I guess this carriage is made for one person on each side. Probably only the king and queen of Zmeykovo have ridden in it before."

"At least our knees aren't touching across from each other," Theo added. "And it's only a short trip by air to our destination."

Theo faced the back of the coach. The two ambassadors who had given him the message mounted the step and grasped the railings.

The carriage flew so fast the landscape below was a blur. Theo tuned in his dragon hearing to the roaring wind, but inside the cabin, everything remained calm, as if they'd never taken off. They landed moments later, without the tell-tale bump of a vehicle hitting solid ground. If engineers could only capture that magical essence, they'd make a fortune in designing aircrafts.

When the messengers opened the carriage doors, Theo, Diva, and Pavel exited. The sun was beginning to set, casting its warm glow onto the protective dome that surrounded the Znahar Tree and Firebird.

"Come in, my friends." Kosara beckoned them forward. "Tangra awaits your arrival."

"But how do we get through the shield?" Theo asked.

The last time anyone had come and gone from it, the priestess had opened a hole in the dome. This time, she provided no entry point.

"You can now pass through, without harm." She came forward and stuck her arm through to the outside. "Tangra has deemed you worthy."

Magda, who was seated by the dome, stood and wiped dirt from her bottom. "About time. She wouldn't let me through without your permission."

"I give you permission." Theo nodded to his aunt and, with Pavel and Diva at his side, stepped through the dome.

Magda followed on their heels, but bounced back when she contacted the barrier. "Ouch."

"Here, let me help you." Theo reached his hand through the dome the way Kosara had, and Magda held on. He drew his arm in slowly, but when Magda's fingers reached the edge, he couldn't pull any farther.

"Kosara, I gave permission," Theo said. "Why can't Magda get through?"

"The tree has protective powers and memories." Kosara laid her hand against the dome. "I have been here a long time, but I know not what makes our sacred tree think she is a danger."

"But, she's a Samodiva, not a Youda. She's Zunitza's sister." Theo looked from Kosara to Magda. "She can't be dangerous."

Magda sulked on the other side. "More likely that Tangra has rejected me—again."

"Theo," Kosara said, "we must perform the ceremony while Tangra's light still shines."

"But Magda … There has to be a way to let her in."

Kosara lowered her head. "Let me see what I can do to allow her entrance for the ceremony since she is important to you."

The priestess approached a group of men dressed in white, hooded robes like the messengers. One left the protective circle and opened the storage section of the carriage. He handed a white robe to Magda, and then returned to his position near the tree.

Magda wrapped the robe around herself and ducked through the dome. "What a moody tree! Theo, thank you for fighting to let me be here with you. Your trust in me warms my heart."

Theo wasn't sure it warmed his to have her here, but unless she proved herself unworthy, he would stand by her.

Magda wrapped herself tighter in the robe. "It's quite chilly here. I vaguely remember this place was full of croaking frogs and other creatures. Now, it's so quiet."

"That's because the creatures know how important today's event is. They keep silent in reverence to the sacred ceremony." Kosara moved to stand by the tree. "As you all know by now, a Golden Apple is born every thousand years. Except for times like this when the Firebird has been murdered. Her rebirth ignites the seed of growth. Only a rightful heir of Zmeykovo may harvest the apple." She turned and beckoned Theo forward. "Your task is to retrieve the apple. You must then return it to the castle and secure it in the Chamber Room."

"Sounds easy enough," he replied.

"Perhaps not," Kosara said. "The apple is under the watchful eyes and protection of the Firebird. You must get past her in order to harvest it. But you'll be fine. We all believe in you." Kosara motioned for everyone to line up in a semi-circle around the tree.

One of the robed men held a willow basket as he approached the group.

"Oh, good. Something to eat. I'm starving," Pavel said, looking with hungry eyes at the basket. "I wonder what kind of fancy stuff they have for the ceremony."

Diva looked into the basket. "Sorry to disappoint you, but they're only dark sun glasses."

Pavel's empty stomach grumbled with an angry voice.

Kosara smiled. "I have prepared a meal for you for after the harvesting."

"I hope I can wait that long." He removed a pair of glasses and placed them over his regular ones, but removed them immediately. "I can barely see anything. These are like what people wear to watch a solar eclipse."

"Without them, you will be blinded," Kosara said. "The Firebird can be brighter than the sun."

"I've been here before when she lit up the sky."

Kosara shook her head. "You have not seen her when her anger arises."

"Just like my mother." Pavel put the dark glasses back on, but slid them down. "I'll put them up all the way when Theo climbs the tree. What about Theo? Doesn't he need some, too?"

"No, a dragon can withstand the extreme light." Kosara turned back to Theo and led him by the hand to a marble slab at the center of the semicircle near the Znahar Tree. "This is your place."

Pavel snickered. "Theo looks like he's going to a spa in that shiny royal robe."

"Shh …" Diva nudged Pavel in the ribs.

"I have one final warning." Kosara held Theo's hands in hers. "The Firebird is not the only danger you'll encounter. The apple itself will tempt your soul. You must resist." She released his hands. "When you're ready, we'll begin the ritual." Kosara's melodic voice soothed Theo, but a tremble had appeared in her words.

Is she nervous or excited? Does she think the apple will tempt me? He still had doubts about being able to rule the kingdom. So much about Zmeykovo's customs remained mysterious to him. If only his father could teach Theo what he needed to know.

He glanced up at the fully ripened apple, high in the tree. It glowed in the fading daylight and made the silver heart-shaped leaves on the branches near it sparkle. *It's now or never.*

"Do you have a ladder?" Theo could easily climb the branches, some of which lay curled against the ground. But was it disrespectful to scramble over the sacred tree?

Kosara shook her head. "You can use any means you need to reach and harvest the apple. Climb, fly, jump—"

Pavel's shout cut off the rest of what Kosara said. "I told ya you might need my rope. I have something else you can try."

Theo turned around as Pavel searched in his backpack. After a while he pulled out a metal object, like a diamond-shaped picture frame with a hole in the middle. He pressed a button, and the metal gadget transformed into a metallic extension with a finger and thumb at the end.

"What is that?" Theo asked.

"An artificial hand, but I don't think I calculated the distance to the apple correctly. I thought it was lower. I'm short about six feet, I guess."

"It reminds me of my grandmother's cane that she uses to get jars down from high shelves."

Kosara laid her hand on Theo's shoulder, and he turned back to look at her. "Young Dragon Prince, this is a sacred ritual. You can use your friend's creation, but you must hurry before Tangra leaves us."

The sun had nearly set, leaving only a faint glow in the sky.

Kosara continued, "The Firebird will be even more protective of the Golden Apple today, since she was destroyed and brought back to life so soon before her normal millennial transformation. You must be cautious. She may try to burn you alive if you look into her eyes. Her beak and talons can rip you to shreds."

"O-okay." Theo breathed deeply to steady his nerves. He could do this. After all the enemies he'd faced since coming to Zmeykovo, having a stand-off with the Firebird should be a breeze.

"One more thing." Kosara motioned toward women, dressed in white robes and holding tiny harp-like instruments. A gentle melody arose as the women plucked the strings.

"The Firebird loves music," Kosara continued. "The soft notes will make her more docile and relaxed."

"I'm ready." Theo exhaled a long breath.

He surveyed the situation. The Firebird was on a branch that lay mere inches above the Golden Apple. The bird's head was tucked under her wing, as if she were dozing. In Selo, Theo had been as light and fast as a squirrel and could scramble up trees and back down in no time at all. Here, he had to climb along only four or five branches to reach the apple.

Grasping the lowest branch, Theo expected resistance from the tree, but apparently the Znahar Tree didn't object to being crawled upon. The bark was cracked and rough on his palms and fingers. He grabbed the next branch and swung himself up as if climbing on his deer. Inch by inch, he slid along the branch as he made his way closer to his prize.

The branch creaked, and the Firebird stirred. Theo looked toward the ground. It was far, but survivable if he fell. *I hope the Znahar Tree isn't so old the branches have rotted on the inside.*

As Theo took another step, the Firebird fluttered her wings and cooed a faint, nervous sound. Theo froze until she settled down once more. The soft notes from the instruments below helped slow his racing heart.

He heaved himself up onto the next branch. With small steps, he swayed as he moved closer to the apple, but was able to grab onto slim branches to steady himself. He paused a moment, surveying the remaining path upward until he decided which branch to tackle next. One more would place him right below the apple.

Once again, he looked down. The distance had increased, but it was still mostly safe. Everyone had their eyes glued to Theo. He almost laughed at the strangeness of seeing them all look like space creatures with the dark glasses.

Can they even see what's going on? Pavel had said he could barely see out of them. Maybe they were like transition lenses, and it took a while to adjust.

The sun still peeked over the horizon, so Theo hadn't failed—yet. He grabbed hold of the next branch. It crackled, and pieces of bark slipped through his fingers.

Theo froze and chanced a look up.

The Firebird had woken. She spread her wings wide and emitted a sound like a cross between a hissing snake and a growling bear. A flash of light brighter than a thousand searchlights engulfed the tree. With one sweep of her wing, the Firebird swatted Theo.

He fell toward the ground so fast that he was certain he'd dent the soil. Never mind all the broken bones he'd suffer.

Someone screamed from below.

No! I can do this. He called on his dragon spirit. *Help me!*

Energy rushed through Theo, piercing his body with electricity. His limbs grew, cracking and stretching, as he shifted into dragon form.

A short pause ensued before Pavel screamed, "Way to go!"

Theo hovered in front of the sparkling Golden Apple. The Firebird made its terrible noise again and blew fire at Theo. He was a dragon. That couldn't hurt—

Ow! He roared and flew out of reach of the bird's flame. The pain was worse than any injury Lamia had inflicted on Theo.

A voice in the back of Theo's mind chuckled, albeit somewhat painfully. "*Keep in mind that she is young, as you are, and extremely powerful after her rebirth.*"

It was true. Theo was like the Firebird. He locked gazes with the magnificent creature. They were both young, venturing out on new exploits, and both desirous of saving their land. The bird had the wisdom of all the other incarnations of it that had preceded, and Theo held the ageless knowledge of his dragon spirit.

His dragon spirit went on, "*She has had to deal with many dragons in the past to keep the apple safe. To her, you are just another thief, a threat.*"

A threat. Theo pondered that. He didn't want to engage in a fire battle with the bird. She was only doing what was expected of her. Theo wasn't even certain a dragon's fire would harm the bird. But it might destroy the apple. He needed another plan. A way to gain the Firebird's trust.

I have it! The one being, besides Kosara, that the Firebird would trust would be another of her own species. Samodivi had the ability to shift into birds. *Can Diva help me, or can I …?*

Theo stared at the Firebird, getting a mental picture. He closed his eyes tight. "*Dragon spirit, please help me change.*"

Once more, Theo's body crackled as he shrank. He opened his eyes. *I'm still flying, so that's a good thing.* He flapped his wings, and fire shot off of the tips. *I did it! I'm another Firebird.*

He flew to the branch where the Golden Apple swayed. The Firebird's roar turned into a coo, her blinding light faded, and she side-stepped toward him, curling her neck around his.

Um. This is awkward.

He wanted to pluck the fruit, but decided to convince the Firebird to let him have it. If she could injure him when he was in dragon form, he had no doubt she could do major damage when he was masquerading as a bird.

"*I need the apple to save your king, my father, Zmey,*" he thought to the Firebird. "*Without it, Lamia and Zlo will continue to destroy Zmeykovo, and the tree you guard will die as well.*"

The bird continued to nuzzle against him.

"*Thank you. I'll take that as a yes. You have my word that I'll protect it with my life.*"

With no more thought, Theo plucked the Golden Apple with his beak. He spread his wings and pushed himself upward, passing through the protective dome. He towered above the Znahar Tree. The last crimson rays of the sun illuminated the apple. Theo let go of the fruit. Somehow, he knew it wouldn't fall to the ground and smash.

The apple twirled in an elegant dance, forming loops so fast that Theo recognized the symbol it made from the streaks of light left behind: the Celestial Turtle. When the apple finished its routine, it twirled in front of him. He grasped the stem in his beak. Slowly, in circles, he descended to the safety of the ground.

Chapter 9
Who's Fooling Whom?

THEO CHANGED BACK to being a boy, fearful the Firebird would continue her courting. The apple he held was delicate and smooth. Even though the sun had set, the fruit still shone. Holding it filled Theo with a strange energy. Joy. Madness. Power. It felt as if he held the universe in his hands. He couldn't tear his eyes away from the glowing golden mass.

Kosara approached him. "Well done, Young Dragon Prince."

Unsure what he was supposed to do with the apple now, Theo handed her the fruit. "I'm glad I won't have to do that again for a thousand years—if ever."

She laughed, and the tree's leaves swayed on the branches, as if sharing a fond memory. "An heir need only harvest the apple once."

"Why did I feel what I did when I was holding it?"

"The apple's power is tremendous." Kosara placed it within the folds of her robe. "Few can withstand the urge to conquer when it is within their grasp. You were wise to present it to me right away. This shows you will be a righteous leader one day."

"How am I supposed to bring it back to the castle if it makes me feel that way?"

"I have a solution." She glided toward the Znahar Tree.

When she left, Diva and Pavel surrounded Theo, while Magda stood off to the side.

Pavel slapped Theo on the back. "That was amazing. You're now Dracoville, the Golden Apple hunter."

"You did great," Diva added, smiling. "It's amazing how that small fruit can make someone rule the entire universe."

Kosara returned. "Yes, indeed. It holds mighty power."

She held a round golden box that sat upon a carved mahogany base. The box itself was cracked throughout, perhaps both by age and by design. In a modernistic way, the segments resembled dragon scales. The lid was topped with a golden figure of the Celestial Turtle.

She handed the box to Theo. "The apple is secure inside. The box will protect you from the apple's pull, so it doesn't affect your mind or your dragon spirit."

The men in white robes approached. One spoke. "Shall we first baptize the apple in the pond?"

"Baptize an apple?" Pavel snickered.

Theo nudged his friend with an elbow and hiss-whispered, "Show some respect."

Kosara spoke to the robed man. "No, this apple is special. The Great Goddess Bendis desires a different ceremony for it. Wait here for my instructions."

The men bowed low and backed away.

To Pavel, Kosara said, "Baptizing the apple purifies its power, but it also weakens it. In the apple's history, only one ruler has partaken of the fruit. When the first Golden Apple blossomed and ripened, it was unknown what the fruit could do to those who consumed it. Our history details the massacres that followed."

"Then …" Theo gulped. "Then shouldn't you do the same for this one? What if I'm tempted to eat the apple?"

"Our deities have determined you are worthy—and almost ready. Your father will be proud of you." A sad smile flitted across Kosara's face. "Darkness surrounds you, and you have more sorrows to undergo first, but we have faith that your suffering will make you stronger." She laid a gentle hand on his shoulder and glided away.

More sorrows? As if he and others here hadn't already suffered enough loss. Was someone else going to die? *Not Zmey, please,* he begged any of their deities who would listen. *We've gone through so much to save him. His people need him. I still need him.*

His father's words came back to Theo: *Promise me you'll always care for our people and land the way I have. I've put them before my own needs.* Theo didn't know how to care for the people. So much here was foreign to him. Diva would be better at this than he would. She had always been a part of this world and its ways. Maybe she thought the same way. She didn't believe Theo could rule Zmeykovo the way it should be. Was that why she wanted to rule?

He mentally slapped himself. *I can't keep thinking that Diva would betray me. She has done nothing to indicate she wants power.*

Even now, the Samodiva was relaxed, talking and laughing with Pavel. No sneaky glances at the apple. No quickly turning away from Theo when he looked her way. She'd always done everything she could to help him learn about Zmeykovo and its residents. Diva wouldn't want to engage in another battle to bring more pain to her world. She loved this land. Her home.

"Earth to Theo." Pavel rapped Theo on the shoulder. "You're going to miss out on the food."

Theo's senses slowly returned to his surroundings. The sounds of life once more filled the pond by the tree. Frogs croaked and jumped from lily pads, sending ripples through the golden water. Fish poked their heads to the surface to snack on unwary insects. Above the water, butterflies fluttered and dragonflies zipped, as if playing a game of tag.

"I'm not hungry. Maybe later."

"Man, you're missing out." Pavel mumbled through a mouthful of amazing smelling bread. He held a plate filled with fresh fruit, more bread, honey, and other items Theo wasn't familiar with.

Theo's stomach gurgled. He broke off a small piece of bread from the plate and popped it into his mouth.

"Hey," Pavel complained.

Two women in white tunics carried silver rhytons toward Theo and Pavel. One looked like it was filled with water and the other with red wine. Pavel held out a ceramic bowl toward the woman carrying the wine.

Theo gave Pavel a chilling look. "Even if they didn't ask if you're twenty-one, it's not okay to drink."

"Okay, my Prince." Pavel mock-bowed. "Stop trying to be my mother. I thought you were my friend."

"Trust me, Pavel. It's for your own good."

"How do you know what's best for me?" Pavel moved his bowl toward the woman carrying the water. He stuffed a handful of grapes into his mouth and grumbled as he walked away, "Everyone has their own view of what's good or bad for themselves."

"Do whatever you want," Theo said, but Pavel had already made it back to the food table.

Theo had thought things would be getting better between the two of them, but apparently Pavel still harbored ill feelings toward Theo. He wasn't sure what to think about anything any longer. He wished he could talk with his human mother and see how she and Nia were doing. The oracle in the pond could tell him. He strolled to the water's edge and sat on the mossy ground, setting the golden box next to him. His heart heavy, he couldn't bear to ask, for fear more of Kosara's predicted sorrows awaited him in Selo. He put his head between his hands and closed his eyes.

Someone sat beside him. Even before she spoke, Theo felt Diva's presence.

"It's a lot to take in, isn't it?" she asked softly.

He looked up. Compassion and strength filled her eyes. She had always been kind and strong. Theo had grown so close to her in his two trips to Zmeykovo. She and the others were more than friends. They were like family to him. He hoped nothing would ever change that. Not his doubts. Not the truth, whatever it turned out to be.

"Yah, it is." He let out a long breath.

They sat in silence for a while, listening to the sounds and feeling the bond between them.

Finally, Theo said, "Will you tell me what Sur said about Magda?"

Diva tensed, looking around. She shook her head and leaned closer. "Not with your aunt always hovering around."

Theo looked for Magda. She stood alone, near the food, but turned her head away from him when he found her. "I think she's just lonely. Everyone treats her as if she has some terrible disease."

"*She's* the disease, Theo. Can't you see that?"

"But she's keeping Zmey alive."

Diva scoffed. "Do you really know that? Or is she doing more damage than good?"

"I know the Samodivi don't trust her, but I think she's changed." Theo *had* to believe his aunt was doing everything she could to save Zmey. If she wanted to harm him, she could have refused to come. Why would she put up all this pretense unless she honestly wanted to protect Zmey?

"Don't you feel her dark powers? Both your dragon and Samodiva abilities have improved so much. Ask your dragon spirit or Zunitza to guide you."

"My mother hasn't said much about her sister." His mother had been quiet lately. Was she saving her energy again to be with Zmey? "I'm sure my mom would have warned me if Magda wanted to harm Zmey or me."

"That's one problem with humans—"

"I'm not human, though," Theo interrupted.

"But you've grown up in the human world. You feel and think like humans."

Theo shrugged. Diva was right. "So, what is the problem with humans?"

"You trust your heart, rather than your instincts."

He thought about that. Was that what set him so far apart from those who lived in Zmeykovo? They relied on the rules of nature. Theo tried to trust his instincts, but his concern for the problems of others—especially many whom he'd met in Zmeykovo—often ended up getting him into trouble. Would he be able to conform to the ways of those who lived here? Rely solely on the ways of nature to rule? Or would he be able to make changes, add in humanitarian aspects and right injustices? Even the Colobar had told Theo that his heart would lead him to the truth.

He sighed. This was all too much to think about. "Let's go back to the castle."

They'd stayed here long enough. Theo had harvested the apple. Kosara had secured it in the box. And Pavel had eaten—hopefully enough to keep him satisfied until they returned. It was time for Theo and Magda to be by his father's side. Theo didn't know how long Ula could keep Zmey alive if he became feverish. After all, she and Sava were the ones who had invited Magda back, despite not liking her.

"Good plan." Magda strode over from the shadows. She cradled a basket tight to her chest. "Kosara helped me pack up food. You didn't eat, and your friend always seems to be hungry."

Kosara glided toward Theo. "Be alert on your journey home. News travels fast. All creatures here are likely to know you have the apple. Many will battle to the death to seize it from you. Your life and that of your friends will be in danger."

More sorrows? Theo looked at his friends. Of course, it would be dangerous. There had been few times that their lives hadn't been in danger. "Maybe we should stay here, at least until morning."

But what would that mean for his father? *Am I going to have to make a choice again, deciding who to protect?*

"No way, Theo!" Pavel shouted. "We all stick together. Those super-sonic fast horsey-dragon things will get us back okay."

Diva remained silent, her face unreadable.

Magda stepped toward Theo. "We have enough magic among us to defeat many enemies."

"I don't know …"

"Oh, come on, Theo." Pavel shook his head. "Don't start this with us. You're not the only one who can protect us."

"Let Theo decide for himself." Magda moved closer. "He is the future ruler. He must learn to make decisions for his people."

"Okay, you're right." Theo stepped away from his aunt and pulled the golden box close to himself. He'd protect it. He had to. "We're a team. I need your support." He looked around the group and added, "And loyalty."

Magda gave him a bitter smile, as if telling him he was in for disappointment from his friends.

The four of them left the protection of the dome and gathered around the carriage. Diva and Pavel entered first, and Diva placed her pouch on the floor.

Theo entered next and was about to close the door when Magda said, "It'll be a bit tight, but I'd like to ride back with you. It's not a long trip, and I do have the food." She waved the basket in front of them.

"Fine with me." Theo moved to the other end of the bench.

"You could leave the food with us," Pavel said at the same time Diva replied, "You can fly. You'd be safe, even at night."

"Yes, I can fly, and I would be safe." She smiled that smile again. "But I prefer to be with my nephew, to help protect him against the monsters of the night."

Magda set the basket on the bench and tore off the white robe, throwing it to the ground. "That nasty rag smells like old goats."

She spun around to settle onto the seat and kicked Diva's pouch. "Oh, so sorry."

The pouch rolled down the carriage steps, scattering its contents. Bottles of herbs and liquids poured out of it. A shiny object caught the glow of the now-risen moon.

Magda stepped out. "Let me put them all back."

Diva scrambled out to collect her scattered belongings. "I can do it myself. You've done enough already."

As Theo and Pavel climbed out of the carriage, Magda held her hand over her mouth as if in shock. She pointed to an object on the ground. "Isn't that my sister's belt?"

Chapter 10
Dark Forces

A SILVER BELT lay a little farther away from the bottles. Nobody moved, but Diva and Magda faced each other with scowls on their faces. Magda glanced toward Theo and gave him an I-told-you-so look. Diva, seeing that, shook her head at both of them.

Hating the conflicting thoughts running rampant in his mind, Theo went to retrieve the silver belt. He rubbed his fingers over the floral designs that decorated its length, all the while wondering what he should say, if anything, and to whom. Magda or Diva?

Before he could do anything, Diva turned away and shoved her possessions back into her pouch. "First time I'm seeing that belt." She shooed Pavel away when he kneeled to help.

"It was in my father's room," Theo said to her back.

"That leaves me out. I've never been in that room," Diva said. "Only one other person here could be responsible."

Theo repeated the words to himself. She'd never been in his father's room. Someone was lying. Magda had said Diva had been looking at the belt earlier in the day. Diva had never lied to him before. Why should she start now? But why would Magda try to cause trouble between Theo and Diva? Was his aunt jealous of his friendship? That seemed childish, or at least an insecure thing to do. Theo wasn't limited to whom he could befriend. If Magda had wanted to be closer to him, he would have gladly allowed it.

"We don't have time to blame each other." Theo clenched his fists. "I don't know what to say and think right now. Everything's so complicated. Let's just get back to the castle and sort everything out. My father needs us."

Diva put the remaining vials into her pouch and pulled the strings tight. She reclaimed her seat, and Pavel joined her on the bench. The last time Theo had seen her so angry was when … Nope. He couldn't remember a time she was this angry. Diva always kept her cool. Something was definitely wrong about this whole situation, but he would get to the bottom of it.

He shook his head and took one last look at the Znahar Tree. Kosara stood silently by the dome. The peace in her face had faded, and sadness gazed back at him. *She must know what's going on, but probably can't say. All the stuff about not tampering with Fate, I'm sure.*

He waved to her after he got into the carriage and sat next to Magda. Kosara gave him a small nod and disappeared into a white mist. She sent silent words to him. *"Theo, I wish you success. May your wisdom and sound judgment accompany and guide you."*

The carriage turned around slowly, but Theo's heart raced. Kosara was wrong. He didn't have wisdom or sound judgment. He'd been tempted to distrust Diva. Why? Because he was weak. He wanted to believe people told him the truth. *But at the expense of believing your friends*, his conscious—or maybe his dragon spirit—scolded Theo.

Theo caressed his mother's belt. *Mom, can you hear me? I'm so confused.*

All was silent, but a soft breeze tickled his cheek.

"I'll take the belt now." That voice wasn't his mother's. It was Magda. "I'll put it back where it belongs."

Theo held on tighter. "No, I'll keep it for now. It'll be safer with me."

Magda jerked her hand back. She ran her fingers over her golden snake bracelet, and its eyes flashed red.

Yes, danger does pour from her, Theo thought. *What game is she playing?*

The carriage sped like a howling wind through the trees. Theo turned away from his aunt and friends to look out the window. He tuned in his dragon senses to his surroundings. The moon's glow danced on the treetops, and silhouettes of creatures darted for cover on the ground or chased after prey. Scratching claws, flapping wings, screeches, and glowing eyes came from below. Blood from fresh kills filled the air. It was not a place he wanted to be.

An engulfing darkness spread over the forest, and the winds picked up. The carriage slowed, as if fighting a force pulling it backward—or downward.

Magda moaned, and Theo turned to see if she was okay. A startled look had crossed her eyes. She knocked on the carriage wall and shouted to the drivers, "What's happening? Keep going. We're not safe here!"

"Yes, we're in a hurry." Theo turned toward the front. "Don't slow down."

"We're trying," a driver shouted, his voice thick with tension. "Some force is fighting us, pulling us toward Tililei Forest."

Pavel paled. "Isn't that … where demons live?"

Theo and Diva nodded.

The friends had traveled there twice already, and that was two times more than Theo cared to have been in the forest. Devil's Throat lay within its bounds, the cave where Sitara had been chained as a Vurkolak. But worse, mind-controlling demons and other monsters roamed free there.

"That's where …" Magda trailed off. "We have to control the winds. Theo? Diva?" She looked from one to the other.

They both shook their heads. Wind was not an element Theo had ever tried to harness.

"I'll see what I can do, then." Magda opened a window.

She closed her eyes tight enough to cause wrinkles around the edges. While chanting words unfamiliar to Theo, she spun her hands around each other as if winding yarn. Theo thought he was going to get dizzy watching her, until she finally shouted and thrust her hands out of the window.

The carriage shot forward as if it were a stone flung from a slingshot.

Magda collapsed onto the bench. Her face had paled and was dripping with sweat. "That's. All. I. Can. Manage."

Seconds later, the carriage boomeranged, traveling twice as fast as before toward the demon forest. The howling winds picked up, snatching the carriage from the sky.

"Theo, you were right." Pavel violently shivered. "We should have stayed with Kosara. I don't … I don't want to go back to that forest again."

Diva squeezed Pavel's hand. "I'll protect you. Both Theo and I will."

"Yes, we won't let the demons get to you. We'll—"

The carriage crashed through the trees. Branches snapped, slapping at the vehicle as they rocketed through the air. Theo released his grip on the side of the carriage, reached over Magda, and slammed the window shut to keep out the debris. Moments later, the carriage pummeled the ground and swayed side to side like a vehicle skidding on ice. With a *bang*, it slammed into a tree.

Dazed, Theo stared at the others, who all had their own shocked faces. A moan at the front of the carriage drew him out of his stupor. Not a demon.

"Someone's hurt." He wrenched open the door and ran to see what had happened.

The Konedrakoni had broken free of their restraints and galloped in circles, colliding with one another, but they refrained from going far from the carriage. Flames accompanied their throaty neighs. One of the coachmen wobbled from the bench, and the two footmen staggered toward the front.

"Are you all okay?" Theo asked. When they nodded, he looked around. "Where's the other driver?"

"Over here." Pavel waved a short distance away from the carriage, where he kneeled by the coachman who lay unmoving on the ground. "Help. He's wounded. I think he's dying."

With narrowed eyes, Diva tossed her pouch to Magda. "Please help the coachman while I calm the animals." Before she dashed toward the first Konedrakus, she added, "Oh, and I *will* check the contents after you return it."

With everyone else occupied, Theo held his sword ready while he scanned the area, looking for immediate danger. Hundreds of yellow eyes blinked throughout the dark forest. The coachmen still appeared dazed, so Theo checked the compartment at the back of the carriage, hoping it held emergency supplies. He found safety equipment and torches. After lighting three of them, he set them around the area. The fire might discourage the advance of the forest creatures—whether demon or animal.

Diva had calmed the dragon-horses by the time Magda finished attending to the wounded man. The uninjured coachmen huddled around the carriage.

"Good news." Magda hurled the pouch back to Diva with more force than Theo thought necessary. "The coachman is fine, just a bump on the head. He only needs a little rest. I think we can get going once the beasts are re-harnessed."

One of the coachmen approached. "Unfortunately, we have bad news. The harness that connects the Konedrakoni to the carriage is busted. We have to fix it." He left and joined the other men.

"We can't stay here too long." Magda darted her eyes around the forest. "These woods are filled with creatures that search for prey at night. They know all our weaknesses."

"Have you been in this part of the forest before, Magda?" Theo asked.

"No, no." Her body trembled. "I only know the forest area around Samodivi Lake. That's all. I never had time to explore Zmeykovo much."

Theo knew that was a lie. Kosara had already indicated that Magda had some connection with the Znahar Tree, and that wasn't too far from this part of Tililei Forest. She was a powerful Samodiva. He doubted that demons terrified her. Something else about the place got on her nerves. Theo would have to figure that out later. Right now, he wanted to check on the damage.

He walked toward the carriage, where the men were conversing. "How long will it take to fix? Is it bad?"

The uninjured driver shrugged. "Half an hour. Maybe a little longer."

"No need to worry, Young Dragon Prince," one of the earlier messengers said. "We have all the parts we need. We'll have you and your friends out of danger in no time."

Theo thanked the men and walked the perimeter around the torches. Just beyond them, yellow eyes blinked and creatures growled. At least for now, they hadn't come closer. He absent-mindedly removed his medallion from under his shirt and rubbed it, feeling warmth radiate from the star.

"What's that?"

Magda's voice right behind him made him jump. *Diva was right. His aunt did lurk around him.* "It's something my mother gave me when she left me in Selo."

"May I see it more clearly?"

Theo didn't remove it from around his neck, but he held the medallion out on his fingertips.

Magda's eyes sparkled. "So that's what happened to it."

"What do you mean?"

"It's part of a twin gift." Magda reached under the neck of her black shirt and pulled out an identical medallion. Well, not quite the same. The words on it were different, but Magda's fingers covered what hers said. "All twins get objects that connect them to one another. Like Lamia's and Zmey's belts. The gifts have powers. And even more when combined."

Theo already knew about the power. His medallion had opened many doors—or should he say portals. And it had done so much more. A niggling thought wormed its way through his brain. He had always thought the medallion was a gift from his mother, something meant for him. But if the medallion was his mother's twin gift, was she the one who was meant to be Zmeykovo's hero? Had she perished because she had given the medallion to him? And then that power or prophecy transferred to him as the new owner and wearer of the sacred object? So many other things he'd been told about the prophecy, however, seemed to point to him being the designated "Unborn Hero" and not his mother.

I wonder if Jabalaka can tell me anything about that? he thought.

Magda stuffed her medallion back into its hiding place. Her eyes remained locked on Theo's medallion until he slid it back beneath his shirt.

"Well, I think we all could use the time to rest." Magda retrieved the basket from the carriage. "Is anyone hungry?"

"I am." Pavel jogged toward her.

That's odd, Theo thought. *Just a little while ago, she was all nervous, and now she's planning a picnic.* Out loud, he said, "I saw blankets in the storage area. I'll get a couple."

He retrieved them and another torch, which he stuck in the ground near the group. Diva took the blankets from him and laid them on the moss. Pavel plopped down next to Magda. She opened the basket and took out food, a stoppered jug of water, and earthenware cups.

Theo and Diva remained standing so they could survey the forest. Theo cast out his dragon senses and was sure Diva was probing the darkness for imminent dangers as well. Sensing nothing overly ominous, he checked on the progress of the carriage work.

Pavel snatched a couple of sandwiches. "Yum. Tasty," he said with his mouth full. "Theo and Diva, come have a bite to eat."

"Yes, you must eat to keep up your strength." Magda held out a tray with an assortment of food. "Theo, come and join us."

"Go," the coachman said, "We'll get this fixed soon enough. Relax with your friends, Young Dragon Prince."

Theo was tired and anxious to get out of there, but he didn't want to eat. It would only upset his churning stomach. "I'm not hungry."

"At least have something to drink," Magda insisted.

He rolled his eyes, but went over to take the ceramic cup she had poured water into. "Thank you." He gulped it down and set the cup on the blanket.

Magda nudged Pavel as he reached for more food and whispered to him. Pavel nodded. He took another cup of water and brought it to Diva. "Please at least have a drink, even if you don't want any food."

Diva took a sip, then dropped the cup to the ground.

"What's the matter?" Theo asked.

"Shh." She nocked an arrow in her bow and crept beyond the glow of the torches. Theo followed, gripping his sword.

The glowing eyes in the forest blinked out, and black furry creatures, looking like giant spiders, leapt from the trees and scampered away.

Something had startled or frightened the forest demons.

Moments later, the pounding of hooves shook the trees. A half-horse, half-man creature galloped straight toward Theo and his friends.

Once again, their enemy Bor Stobor had come to engage in battle.

Chapter 11
Creatures of the Night

BRANDISHING A MACE, Bor Stobor hissed as he approached, but he stopped before reaching his goal. He looked around as if waiting for someone. Theo wondered why his dragon senses hadn't smelled the offensive odor of Bor Stobor's body well before he arrived. The forces within the demon forest must have masked his approach. Now, the Karakonjul's powerful dung odor made Theo nauseous.

"Why aren't you guarding your precious bridge, Karakonjul?" Theo held his sword ready to attack.

"I go where my master commands." Bor Stobor dug deep grooves in the ground, and his tail covered with silver dragon scales swished with loud slaps against the beast's body. "My bridge isn't the most precious thing in Zmeykovo right now. My army and I are here to take it from you."

Theo tightened his grip on his sword. *"Army,"* he thought to Diva. *"More troops are coming. Or do you think the Karakonjul is trying to intimidate us?"*

"Probably both," she thought back. *"We can defeat them either way once he makes a move."*

When Theo had been captive in Kaleto Fortress, he had discovered he could talk with Diva mentally. This was the first time since then that they'd needed to use that ability. He was thankful they still could communicate this way.

"I need to get to the Golden Apple to keep it safe. I left it in the carriage." Theo cast a glance to the side.

Pavel had dropped his sandwich and was sneaking toward the carriage.

Good, Theo thought, *he'll be safer inside. At least, I hope.*

But Pavel came back out, holding both his and Theo's backpacks. He gave Theo a thumb's up, then snuck back closer to Magda.

"It looks as if Pavel took care of that problem," Diva thought to Theo.

Theo, Diva, and Bor Stobor stood at a stalemate for several moments. The coachmen had dropped their tools and taken up spears. The men surrounded Pavel and Magda, but Theo's aunt took her stance among them.

Once again, Theo was relieved that Pavel would be protected. He and Diva could concentrate on Bor Stobor.

More sounds filled the forest. The flapping of wings. And another stench permeated the air. The Harpies with their gore-coated bodies had entered the scene. Their hisses and shrieks came from every direction.

Other creatures joined the growing cacophony. The baby-like Navi. The Mori, with their human soul trapped within a demon one. The miniature green dragons. The half-goat, half-human beings. Others Theo hadn't yet encountered. And at the back, torches flared and glinted on the swords of the Knights of Darkness, the traitorous soldiers who had once sworn fealty to Zmey.

There was nowhere to run. *"Will this be our last battle?"* Theo thought to Diva.

"I'm not planning to die today," she thought back. *"We've faced terrible odds before and have survived."*

Bor Stobor, a smug look on his filthy face, pranced forward a step. He held up his mace, as if telling his army to wait for his signal.

"Oh, Mighty Dragon Prince." The Karakonjul laughed and mock-bowed. His one red eye in the center of his monstrous head glared at Theo. "We have you surrounded. It's useless to resist. I've been told you're smart, although I've never seen that side of you."

Theo's dragon spirit clawed to be released, but Theo held him back.

"Theo," Diva thought to him, *"keep him talking as long as you can. I have a plan."*

"Will do," he thought back. To Bor Stobor, Theo said, "If you're here to join our picnic, I don't think Magda brought enough food."

"Food." The horse-man snorted. "We'll eat you and your friends. The Harpies are starving for some fresh meat."

"That leaves you out. You don't smell fresh at all."

"Theo!" Diva scolded him in his mind. *"Keep him talking. Don't antagonize him to attack yet."*

"Sorry," he thought back. *"But it's the truth."*

She shook her head at him.

"Just as I said. Not bright at all." Bor Stobor's tail swished faster. "Just look at my horde. You have no chance of victory. But you do have a chance to live if you hand over the Golden Apple."

"The what?" Theo glanced over to Magda. "Did you pack any apples? This stinky horse wants one."

Bor Stobor thrust his mace to the side. "I don't see it on the prince. Search the carriage. Demolish it if you have to. I want that apple found."

A stampede of hoofs shook the ground as the half-goat creatures advanced on the carriage. The Konedrakoni breathed fire on them. Shrieks and burned flesh filled the night. Theo turned to help, but there were too many. The creatures jumped and pranced on the carriage, running into and out of the doors, as if playing tag. The assault was over almost as soon as it began, leaving the carriage in ruins.

"Enough games!" Bor Stobor shouted. "Where is it? Do you really want to die for an apple?"

"We don't have it." Theo stood his ground, although his insides quivered. "We left it with Kosara. Do you think they'd really trust *me* with the apple?" Theo hoped his bluff worked.

The Karakonjul growled. "I've had enough. I don't care if she told me not to kill you. You're going to die, along with your Samodiva friend." Bor Stobor shrieked, raised his mace, and swung it in circles as he galloped forward.

Chaos ensued. Creatures of the night swarmed Theo and his friends.

Theo didn't know what Diva's plan was, but now was a good time to implement it. Arrows zipped past Theo as Diva released her weapons. Screams of the dying echoed within the darkness of the forest. The coachmen thrust their weapons at anyone who came near, coating spears with blood. Magda threw out her hands in a circular motion. Gale-force winds swept the attackers back.

Theo drew his silver sword and charged toward Bor Stobor. Their weapons clashed, sending vibrations all the way to Theo's shoulders. He pulled back and aimed for the Karakonjul's chest.

A beating of what sounded like thousands of wings drowned out the clamor of battle. Innumerable bats descended from the trees. The creatures swarmed Bor Stobor and the attacking army. Beings shrieked as claws and thirsty teeth sank into their flesh. The enemy army retreated into the darkness, a dark mass of bats pursuing them.

Only Bor Stobor remained. He hurled his mace around him, but the bats clung on. "Luck's on your side this time, Mighty Dragon Prince, but we'll meet again." Swinging his mace, he galloped after his retreating army.

The battle was over almost before it began.

Dazed, Theo shook his head. *What just happened? Was that Diva's plan?* Time to ask after he checked on everyone. He rushed toward Pavel. "Are you okay?"

Pavel stood on shaky legs. "F-fine. That was intense."

Theo examined the others. Magda and the coachmen hadn't received any injuries other than those from the carriage crash.

"Where did Diva go?" he asked. The last he'd seen of her she'd been shooting arrows.

"I'm here." She stepped out of the forest, her bow once more free of weapons. "I followed the army to make sure they kept going."

Theo gave her a hug. "That was a great plan of yours. Calling the bats."

"That wasn't me. I called for any birds nearby, but friendly ones don't dare venture here."

"If it wasn't you …" Theo sent out his dragon senses, but the vicinity remained quiet. "Who would have called them?"

She shrugged. "I have no idea, but we should get out of here as soon as we can."

The coachmen had left the group and gathered around the carriage. One spoke. "We're not going anywhere in this any time soon."

The carriage lay in pieces, trampled by the goat people.

Theo looked around the group. The Konedrakoni hadn't deserted them in the battle. "We'll have to leave the carriage, but I think we have enough other ways to get out of here. Diva and Magda can shift into birds to fly. I can change into a dragon and carry Pavel. The Konedrakoni look like they could each carry two people."

The coachmen shook their heads and one said, "They have not been trained to carry personnel, only pull the carriage. I fear they would toss us to the ground or burn us to crisps if we tried."

"Maybe I can carry all of you." Theo's dragon form had only borne one person on his back at a time before. He was strong. Five shouldn't be too many.

Theo closed his eyes and sought his dragon spirit. *Let's do this.*

He stretched his shoulders. A rush of heat filled him, and power pulsed through his body. Theo's pores opened, breathing in the magic of his surroundings. His legs and arms thickened, and he dropped to the ground on all fours. Next, his body stretched. Red scales erupted everywhere. Majestic wings sprouted. Heat filled every inch of his body.

Theo opened his eyes and stretched his wings, creating a breeze. Crouching as low to the ground as he could, he spoke to Diva's mind, *"Please tell them all to get on."*

Diva relayed his message.

Pavel ran his fingers along the red scales as he climbed up. "Man, I wish you could talk with me the way you do with Diva."

The coachmen bowed first before approaching, reverence shining in their eyes. Even Magda had a look bordering on awe, but one tinged with fear and jealousy.

Diva whispered to his mind, *"You're a beautiful dragon. One with the courage of an army."*

Her praise made guilt burn his soul. He'd been convinced to doubt her friendship and loyalty. Diva would never do anything to betray him. He had to trust his heart, not the convincing words of others.

With all his passengers holding on, Theo stood. The weight made his legs wobble. He stretched his wings to limber them. Gentle flapping soon became thrusts. He took several running steps forward and leapt into the air.

Only to fall back to the ground.

Theo tried again, running as far as he could before lifting into the air.

Once more, he failed to gain altitude.

Weariness overcame him. Panting, he laid his head on the ground. *I shouldn't feel this tired.*

He rose and readied himself to run again.

"Theo, stop. It's too much." Pavel slid off of Theo's back, and the coachmen followed.

"*Back to normal*," Theo said to his dragon spirit.

As his body reshaped to human form, he thought about the time he tried to fly with the mechanical wings Pavel had made. That seemed ages ago. Theo had been so filled with hope and wonder back then. So young and naïve. Zmeykovo had changed so much about him.

He'd killed here. At home in Selo, he'd never been able to hurt anything.

He'd lied here. Of course, he'd told fibs at home. What boy didn't? But, in Zmeykovo, were his white lies uttered to protect his friends or himself? Did he need to make himself seem stronger and smarter than he really was?

He'd failed his friends here. Not once. Not just today. But over and over again. In Selo, Theo would never have thought of mistrusting his friends.

"Sorry," Theo said once the transformation was complete. "I really thought I could carry you all."

Diva came to his side and helped Theo up. "You did your best. We can all take turns standing guard while the coachmen fix the carriage. I doubt Bor Stobor will be back tonight."

The flapping of wings approached again.

"What now?" Theo barely held his sword aloft. He was so drained. More tired than he'd been in a long time. He lacked the energy to fight any longer.

The swirling mass of bats had returned. Had they devoured Bor Stobor and his army and were now coming to finish off the rest of them?

The bats spun like a funnel, spinning fast as they touched the ground. The blackness took the shape of a man, wearing a cloak as dense as the darkest night.

Chapter 12
Deadly Song

SPARKS SHOT OFF of the man—creature?—as he moved closer. His silent strides were those of a predatory stalker. Beneath a hooded cloak, long strands of black hair peeked out, but the man's face remained hidden. The handle of the man's long black sword was shaped like bat wings. An intricate design of lines and circles embellished the blade.

Despite his exhaustion, Theo held his sword steady and stepped in front of his friends. "That's far enough. Who are you and what do you want?"

The dark-cloaked figure continued to approach.

Theo swung his sword, but the enemy dodged the blow with inhuman speed. Once more, Theo jabbed toward the man, but he disappeared. Frustrated and growing tired, Theo whirled around, sensing a presence behind him, and faced his adversary.

"Is that any way to treat the person who rescued you?" The man's voice was deep, soothing, lulling victims into a sense of security.

Theo shook away the effect and pointed his sword toward the man's heart. "I'll ask again. Who are you and what do you want?"

The man bowed his head. "I am Drakus, the lord of darkness, at your service."

He flipped back his hood, revealing deep-set black eyes and a pale face, except for slightly ruddy cheeks. His nose was long and straight, but had only one nostril.

"Are you another demon coming for the Golden Apple?" Theo asked.

"A demon, sadly, yes." Pain crossed the man's eyes. "But I don't want or need the apple. I already have eternity and enough power to overcome my enemies."

"Then what do you want?"

Drakus came closer, his sad smile revealing sharp incisors. "I desire to help you."

Theo stepped back. Those teeth … Drakus had to be a vampire. Theo shuddered and rubbed his neck. "How do you even know we need help?"

"Who other than an heir to the throne would be conveying the Golden Apple?" Drakus circled Theo. "I know it all. Who you are. Why you're here. I, too, want to defeat your aunt Lamia. She has caused me eternal suffering. I want revenge."

"What did she do to you?"

The muscles in Drakus' face tightened, and his eyes hardened. He leaned forward his words came out with a hiss. "She deprived me of my love, and she made me into this." He swept his free hand down his body. "An Oupir. A beast of the night."

"How can you help us?"

Drakus touched the blade of his sword. "Beasts don't fear weapons. They fear other monsters. I have the power of a thousand men. And more 'gifts' than either your father or aunt."

"Is controlling the wind one of them?" Something had pulled them down to this spot, where it was convenient for Drakus to meet them.

"Yes." Drakus smiled. "I see you are wise. It was not for a nefarious purpose. I merely discerned your presence and knew this would be my one opportunity to join forces with you."

Theo used his dragon senses to try to peer into the man's soul. He found nothing. Did the undead retain their souls? The man could have caused them all harm, but he hadn't. Theo wanted to trust Drakus, give him a chance.

Drakus, as if perceiving Theo's doubt, continued, "Bor Stobor's army couldn't stop me. I can immobilize your enemy, so you can strike the fatal blow."

Theo wasn't certain he wanted to kill Lamia. At least not now. He'd wait until he could return the ouroboros belt to Zmey. He had no idea what the backlash would be if he killed her before then. The two parts of the belt were so intertwined that bringing about Lamia's death now might escalate his father's demise as well. Theo could wait a little longer—and maybe even leave Lamia's death or punishment for Zmey to decide.

But what about Drakus' offer? Having additional support to fight their enemies would be welcome, especially since they lost Zima.

Theo didn't want to make this monumental decision on his own. Could he trust Drakus? The man's anger toward Lamia felt genuine, but did he harbor some other ulterior motive?

"Give me a moment, please." Theo turned to look at his companions. None had moved since Drakus' arrival, but they all kept their weapons poised toward the Oupir. Even Pavel had found and sharpened a stick. A stake? Theo hoped it was hawthorn. Stories told how that was the most effective wood to kill a vampire. In a pinch, maple or ash would do.

Feeling the Oupir's stare against his back, Theo met with his friends. "What do you all think? Should we let Drakus join us?"

"Most definitely not!" Magda responded first. Her voice quavered, and she'd grown pale. "Demons are not to be trusted."

Diva spoke next. "I feel hurt, anger, pain from him, but no malice toward us. I say if he wants to assist, then we should let him."

Theo looked at Pavel next. His friend's eyes were wide, and he trembled. "I guess I'll trust Diva's judgment. But, man, he's creeping me out."

Only the coachmen remained to comment. Theo said to them, "I know you won't be part of our fighting group going forward, but what's your opinion?"

Almost as one, the men replied, "We trust in your decision, Young Dragon Prince."

Theo sighed. That wasn't helpful, but he'd made up his mind. He, too, felt Drakus would be more of an asset than a hindrance. Theo's heart told him he could trust the Oupir. He strode back to Drakus.

"We will value your assistance—and friendship." Theo held out his hand. "It seems we have similar goals."

Drakus grasped Theo's hand in a firm handshake. It was warm, not cold as he had expected.

"I must become acquainted with the scent of each of your companions," Drakus said. "There are those in Zmeykovo who can appear disguised as others. I must ensure I encounter no trickery."

Theo knew all about that. Bor Stobor's shape-shifting abilities had already caused enough damage.

Theo led the Oupir toward the group and made introductions. "This is Pavel."

Drakus drew closer and sniffed Pavel's neck, causing him to shiver. "No need to worry. I'm not thirsty for blood. I'm thirsty for revenge. And, besides, I've already eaten. The Karakonjul provided me with a fine feast."

"You ate Bor Stobor?" Pavel's voice rose.

"Not him, the dung that clung to him. It is what attracted me to this area in the first place."

Pavel covered his mouth. "You eat … manure?"

"Unfortunately, that is part of my curse." Drakus sighed. "When I cannot find other sustenance, I must nourish myself with the refuse of others. Drinking blood is a last resort."

"We have real food." Pavel pointed to the basket. "Take what you need."

Theo couldn't help but smile. He'd never seen Pavel so willing to share food with anyone.

Drakus licked his lips with his barbed tongue. "I shall, later. Thank you." He turned toward Diva and sniffed. "Oh, a lovely Samodiva. You have a familiar scent."

"We've been in this forest before," she replied.

He pursed his lips. "Perhaps that's it."

"And this is Magda." Theo pointed toward his aunt.

Drakus sniffed and walked around her. "Another Samodiva. You, too, have a scent I recognize. You were here long ago, with another basket, perhaps?"

Magda pulled her arms close to her chest. With her eyes lowered, she shook her head. "I've never been to this forest. And I've only recently returned to Zmeykovo. It had to have been someone else."

Drakus put his finger to his mouth. "Perhaps you are right. Forgive my confusion."

"These other men are—" Theo started.

"Ah, yes, I know of these men well." Drakus bowed. "Priestly ambassadors of Tangra. How I miss the warmth of His light. My curse allows me to be awake only between noon and midnight. During daylight hours, I must hide within the shadows. This dense forest provides a safe haven, since it allows little light to pass through."

The men acknowledged Drakus with their own bows. They returned to work on the carriage. Their spokesperson addressed Theo. "We will work all night to repair the damage. Two will repair the carriage while the other two stand guard."

"Let me offer my hospitality as an alternative," Drakus said. "My home is not luxurious, but it will shelter everyone from other predators."

Theo hesitated. The day had been long, and he was exhausted. Pavel looked just as tired. It was obvious they weren't going to make it back to the castle tonight. He worried about his father. Magda had left Ula to care for him, but what if something bad happened again?

He turned to his aunt. "Will you—?"

She cut him off. "Zmey will be okay. Ula knows what to do."

"Maybe you should return to make sure. The rest of us can look out for each other."

While casting a sidelong glance at Drakus, Magda shook her head. "No, I should stay here with you. I have powers to protect you if any more danger appears."

Theo looked at Diva, and she shrugged but nodded. The night *was* incredibly dark. More demons lurked outside the bounds of the torches. They hadn't yet tried to feed on everyone's weaknesses and fears, but how long would the creatures resist?

"Thank you." Theo retrieved his backpack from Pavel. "We'll accept your offer."

The coachmen collected the pieces of the carriage and followed behind Theo and the others, who carried the torches. The Konedrakoni trotted behind everyone, breathing fire at the demons snarling within the forest. None came too close. A worse predator guarded their potential prey.

They trekked after Drakus for a short while, stopping when he held up his hand.

"You're now entering more dangerous territory." Drakus motioned for everyone to gather around him. He whispered, "My abode is beyond the great oak you see up ahead. Complete silence is required until we have gone past that tree. I will signal when we have reached the safety of my residence."

"What's in the tree?" Pavel's voice shook.

"The birds of paradise live there: Alkonost, Sirin, and Gamayun," Drakus said. "Tonight, only Sirin is here, and she currently slumbers. You must not wake her."

"What will happen if we do?" Theo asked.

"She will sing."

Pavel laughed, but then slapped his hand over his mouth to suppress the noise. "Does she sing terribly? Every bird I've ever heard was nice to listen to."

"No, she has a beautiful voice. She is a goddess." Drakus had a faraway look in his eyes. "She herself is a lovely maiden, with wings and the lower half of her body that of a bird."

"Is she a Harpy?" Pavel asked.

"No, she is beautiful, and her intentions are good."

"Why is her song dangerous?" Theo asked. The story was fascinating, but exhaustion was claiming him, and he wanted to find a safe place to rest.

"She is called the 'Bird of Joy' and is associated with good luck, while Alkonost is the 'Bird of Sorrow,' and Gamayun is the 'Bird of Prophecy.' "

Pavel scrunched up his face. "But you said we have to worry about Sirin. It sounds like we should be more afraid of Alkonost, and she's not here."

"It's true that Sirin's songs are those of joy, but they come with severe consequences." Drakus paused to take a deep breath. "Only those who are happy can hear her songs. They transport the listener to a blissful state."

"That still doesn't—"

"Let me finish." Drakus held his hand up to Pavel. "Sirin rewards those who are virtuous with her song. However, anyone who hears the melody immediately forgets about everything else. He'll follow the bird to the ends of the world until he dies. His mind will never again be his own."

Pavel's mouth formed a wide "O," but no sounds came out.

"Some say," Drakus continued, "that her singing is a way to join the spiritual and physical. It signifies a person's union with Heaven at the moment of death. When the soul hears the beautiful music, it forgets everything else and willingly leaves the body. A proverb about Sirin goes 'When she raises up her voice in song, she no longer feels her own self.' The same thing happens to anyone who hears her song. He loses his awareness of himself in order to experience the delights of paradise."

Drakus paused again. "You are young. I assume your soul does not yet yearn for paradise."

Pavel shook his head so violently that his glasses slid down his face. "No, no, no. I get it now. Let's get going. I'll be quiet."

Theo peered toward the tree and enhanced his dragon vision. "I don't see a bird-woman there. Are you sure she's around?"

"See that owl?" Drakus pointed. "That's her. She doesn't always appear as half-woman, half-bird."

Theo couldn't help but think that maybe Drakus was leading them into a worse trap than remaining outside in the forest. It was too late now. It was a better choice to face one monster rather than thousands. Sirin might not be a Harpy, but those other bird-women lurked in the forest out of his sight. He knew they had returned and were there, waiting, by the smell of carrion, which coated their bodies.

"I agree with Pavel," Theo said. "It's time to go. We need to get out of the forest."

Theo scrutinized every step he took, using his dragon senses to ensure he didn't step on anything that would make noise. Pavel held a torch at an angle, so it illuminated the space directly in front of him. Everyone else used their own precautions.

A branch snapped.

Theo stopped moving and held his breath. It hadn't been him. Everyone else had frozen, too.

The night became deathly quiet. A flutter of wings came from the oak. Then the most beautiful song Theo had ever heard filled the air.

Chapter 13
A Dark Lair

TIME FROZE. Gentle notes surrounded Theo on tendrils of the breeze. They caressed his body, his mind, his soul. The soft voice reminded him of his adoptive mother, singing to him when he was a little boy in Selo. Peace flowed through him. Joy. Love. Belonging. Along with something else. Tugging within his body prevented him from advancing. A fierce roar in his mind. It felt as if his blood had heated to the boiling point.

"Fight back, Theo!"

Who had said that?

Time restarted.

Chaos broke out. Screaming. Flailing against restraining arms. Chanting comforting words.

A whoosh of air almost knocked Theo to the ground. Everything came flooding back, taking his breath away.

"Dragon spirit," he begged, *"mute the song."*

Silence. Blissful quiet.

Theo was going to be okay, but what about everyone else? Magda and the coachmen stood beyond the oak, their faces pale, but apparently within the safe zone Drakus had spoken about. Pavel had made it halfway to the tree. Diva and Drakus both strained to hold him back.

If the song was that strong, who had prevented Theo from advancing?

"*We're a team.*" His dragon spirit had kept Theo safe.

"*How can we save Pavel?*"

"*Enter his mind,*" Theo's dragon spirit replied. "*Remind him of all that is good in his life. Everything the two of you have shared. The friendship. The adventures. Even the struggles that bound you to one another for life. You will create an even stronger bond.*"

Theo rushed over and faced his friend, blocking his view of the tree. Pavel's eyes were unseeing, or perhaps seeing something from another place. "Stay with us, pal."

With his eyes squeezed tight, Theo pushed his thoughts into Pavel's mind. Instead of the jumble of formulas and gadgets Theo had expected to find, he discovered his friend sitting under the oak they now tried to keep him from reaching.

"Hey, Pavel." Theo sat next to his lifelong friend. "It's time to get going."

Pavel looked up. A blissful smile radiated from his face. "Theo! Hey, man. Glad you're coming with me. Think of all the fun we can have together."

"I don't think we can get into any kind of trouble or mischief where you're headed."

"No?" A fleeting look of sorrow flashed in Pavel's eyes. "I guess that's okay. We do have to grow up sometime."

"Nah, not yet. Besides, I don't think you'll be able to invent anything new if you leave us now."

Pavel's body began to slump. "Ah, man."

Theo kept speaking, not wanting to lose his best friend. He reminded Pavel of his family. How his mother would cry if he never came home. How his older brother would inherit all of Pavel's possessions and likely just throw them away.

"Not my Paveltron!" Pavel whimpered.

"Especially your Paveltron," Theo said.

Theo recounted every adventure he and Pavel had shared, both in Selo and in Zmeykovo. The mechanical wings Pavel made. Crossing the rickety bridge where Pavel almost fell. Visiting Baba Yaga for cures. Theo talked about how they'd always been there to support each other. He spoke about all the trouble they got in, but how much fun it had been anyway.

"We'll never have that again if you don't stay."

"But the song is so beautiful," Pavel said.

"Who will take care of Whirl if you leave?"

"My Whirl?" Pavel turned wide eyes toward Theo. "I can't leave him."

"And Diva's not going to be where you're heading."

"No Diva?"

Theo said whatever else he could think of to bring Pavel back. With each word Theo spoke, Pavel's blissful state deteriorated. The oak tree began to shed its leaves, and the bark started to flake. The glorious song began to turn sour.

Theo sang along with it.

Pavel covered his ears. "Hey, man. That sounds awful, and you're messing up the words."

The tree roots shriveled, and the oak crumbled into ash. Last of all, Pavel faded away, and Theo pulled himself out of his friend's mind.

Theo stood looking into Pavel's eyes. The glazed look had disappeared. Now, only sorrow filled them.

"Welcome back. I thought we were going to lose you." Theo wrapped his arms around Pavel and squeezed him tight. This was not time for a back-slapping man hug. His friend deserved a full body-crushing embrace.

Pavel didn't look relieved. "It's gone. The beautiful song is gone."

Diva joined Theo in the hug. "I'll sing for you again. When Sur's around. I'll teach you how to make the harp, too, so you can play your own tunes on Whirl."

Pavel's face brightened. He returned his friends' hugs.

"Come on," Diva said. "Let's get out of here and go to Drakus' home."

They crossed the boundary onto Drakus' property, and all the tension that had built up in Theo vanished. He felt Pavel relax, too. The danger was over, and Theo didn't have to worry that his friend would abandon them to return to Sirin's tree.

Theo wondered how Diva had withstood the song. The answer came swiftly. She'd had many years to hone her abilities, unlike Theo who had only recently been developing his. It also made sense that the song wouldn't affect the undead, so Drakus had been fine. The others, Magda and the coachmen, must have had their own way of fighting Sirin's song.

"*Or* some *may not have heard it*," his dragon spirit suggested. "*The song is for the happy and virtuous*."

Theo looked at Magda. His aunt held her arms tight around her waist. Perhaps the song had bothered her after all.

Drakus walked a little farther and stood in front of a tall stone with a cross carved into it. His tomb? Theo shivered. The Oupir pulled a metal ring, and the heavy stone door opened.

The coachmen excused themselves, saying they would remain outdoors to fix the carriage. They would be safe enough in the enclosure, with the Konedrakoni warning them of any danger.

Warmth embraced Theo as he entered. He had expected the room to be a cold crypt, housing only a coffin situated on a platform in the center of the small room. It did have Drakus' coffin, but that sat off to the side, the lid closed. Pavel, at least the boy he used to be, would probably say that Drakus had made his bed. On the wall above the coffin was a painting of a dark-haired man and a beautiful woman.

Candles scattered along the floor gave the room a soft glow, as did the blazing fireplace, which Pavel sat at, warming his hands. The structure's design was Gothic, made of smooth black stone. Snarling from each side of the mantel was an enormous black carved bat. Claws reached down the side, and folded wings trailed up the wall. The creature's red eyes and sharp teeth made it look as if it were ready to jump off of its perch and attack its prey. Theo was glad it wasn't a living being. Also creepy were stuffed black cats that stood with arched backs on the hearth.

The room even held a small bookcase, filled with leather-bound tomes. Diva had already made her way over to those, flipping through the pages. If it weren't for the cats, bats, and casket, the room would have been cozy.

Theo turned toward his host, discovering the Oupir's staring gaze. Yah, that was creepy, too. Theo couldn't help but ask the question on his mind. "You were buried with all of this?"

Drakus chuckled. "No, it was just the coffin in the ground, with the stone slab outside covering the grave. I managed to dig my way out, regardless."

"How did you get here, then?"

"Let's see. It was so long ago." Drakus tapped his fingers against his lips. "Villagers were terrified when they discovered me, alive, causing mischief. It wasn't anything terribly bad. More things like breaking their dishes or smearing manure onto their homes—but only on those of people I'd disliked while living."

Theo nodded. "I know boys in my own village who do stuff like that now while they're alive."

"Anyway," Drakus continued, "the villagers were going to decapitate me to prevent me from getting out of my grave. Since I'd never truly completely died—"

"What?" Theo stammered.

"Hold on. I'll get to that in a moment." Sadness filled the Oupir's eyes. "To prevent myself from having my head cut off and being dead for eternity, I dug up my coffin and moved it and the slab into Tililei Forest, where I knew none of the villagers would ever venture voluntarily. I found this small cave and have been slowly making it homier."

Theo waited for Drakus to broach the other topic, but the man seemed lost in his own sadness. Theo would have to ask again because he was too curious to let the subject go. "So, how is it you're not completely dead?"

Drakus blinked. "Ah, yes, that. Do you know about the soul's journey after death?"

Theo nodded. When a person died, their spirit left the body and traveled for forty days, visiting all the places that meant something to them during their lifetime. At the end of forty days, some wanted to return to life, but discovered their body had begun to decay. That was enough to turn them away, and they made the last leg of their journey to the otherworld, the land of the dead. But Drakus' body was still whole, not decaying. He'd suffered a different fate.

"Good. Good to know," Drakus said. "That much less to have to explain. It's rather simple, I must say. When I died, my spirit refused to leave my body. I never traveled through the world those forty days. I had other unfinished business to attend to."

Theo could guess where this was going. "Lamia?" he said.

"Yes, that beast destroyed my life." Drakus grabbed one of the stuffed cats and squeezed so hard the animal burst open. "She's the reason I'm this way. Worse than that, she made my beloved Lora into a beast as well."

Bloody tears lined the rims of Drakus' eyes.

Theo asked, "Is she an Oupir, too?"

"No, worse." Drakus gazed at the painting above his coffin. "She's out there. My sweet, beautiful Lora followed me here and refuses to leave. But she can never enter my protective area."

Theo tried to imagine what beast in the forest Lora had been turned into. Then it hit him. "She's Sirin, isn't she?"

Drakus nodded, his head hung low. "And Alkonost and Gamayun were two of my wife's best friends, who got trapped in the curse."

"Why would Lamia do that?" Theo understood why his aunt hated him, but what purpose would turning Drakus into an Oupir and his wife into Sirin serve Lamia?

"Why?" Drakus' maniacal laughter chilled Theo. "Lamia didn't need a reason. An insult, no matter how small, was all it took in those days for her to torment people. She has no soul."

Theo sometimes wondered if that was true. When he'd killed her a year ago, she'd transformed into a beautiful woman. In death, she'd appeared peaceful, no longer evil. Theo wasn't certain that that would be the case if—no when—he destroyed her again. Had all goodness departed from his aunt when Zlo resurrected her?

"I'm weary. Midnight approaches, and I must enter my coffin." Drakus stretched his shoulders. "Get comfortable for the night. There are blankets by the bookshelf. As I said, it's not opulent like the dragon castle, but suitable for sheltering you tonight."

"Have you been to the dragon castle?" Theo asked.

"Many, many years ago. But that's another story for another time." Drakus bowed and walked over to his coffin. "I shall know where to find you when you are ready to defeat the real monster of Zmeykovo." With that, he lifted the coffin cover, crept inside, and closed the lid.

Theo was exhausted, too, but he wanted to check to see how Pavel was doing. Both his friends were sitting on the hearth, and Pavel was examining a paper. Theo looked around for Magda, but she wasn't inside. He shrugged. The coachmen and Konedrakoni were outside. She'd be safe enough out there.

He approached his friends. "Hey, guys. How are you doing?"

Diva smiled, and Pavel looked up. He'd lost the anxiety and anguish that had been plaguing him since Zima's death. Maybe Sirin had done some good after all.

"Hey, Theo. Thanks for rescuing me. That was some crazy stuff, wasn't it?"

"Sure was." Theo moved aside metal and glass pieces of a device that surrounded Pavel and sat on the edge of the hearth. It made Theo happy that Pavel was working on a new gadget. The boy Theo had known was slowly starting to return. "What are you making?"

"A special communications device. I'm calling it a Dracophone. I'm hoping to use it to call home." Pavel showed Theo the schematic, but none of it made sense to him.

When Theo and Pavel had been in Selo, the only way the Rusalki from Zmeykovo could contact them was through a mermaid's shell. This wouldn't help him or Pavel connect with the human world, though. How would they get the shell to their families?

"Can you explain in simple terms how it'll work?" Theo didn't hold out much hope that he'd understand what Pavel said, but he wanted to see the return of his friend's enthusiasm for inventing.

"Sure!" Pavel's eyes brightened. "It's a point-to-point device between two dimensions. I found some cool stuff in the treasure room that I think will actually make it work. I hope you don't mind that I took them." Worry crossed Pavel's face.

"Nah, not at all. Use what you need. There's certainly plenty of stuff there."

"Great." Pavel picked up a couple of items from the hearth. "I found this nifty dragon scale." He handed it to Theo to inspect.

The black scale with a purple sheen made Theo shiver. Lamia's mother had been a black dragon, and Lamia had used her scales to cover the book of secrets.

"That's the heart of the device," Pavel said as Theo handed the scale back. "I want to use it to channel energy that will create a connection between Selo and here. And this"—Pavel held out a large emerald—"will open both portals."

Theo nodded, not having a clue how any of that would work.

"Anyway," Pavel continued, "once I establish a connection, it creates a hologram and interface like Facetime."

"How'd you come up with the idea?"

"I found a scroll in the treasure room that had a bunch of neat images on it," Pavel said. "Diva explained the words to me. I think someone here tried to make something similar. I'm just attempting to finish what they started."

Theo examined the paper once more, but still couldn't make heads or tails of how it might work.

Pavel added, "This is only a basic idea. I need more parts to make it work. When I get them, I'll show you a prototype."

"That would be great to contact our families. It seems like we've been gone for years."

Pavel had to be thinking about his family as much as Theo was about his own. Nia and his mom knew where Theo had gone, but Pavel hadn't told his family. Did they find out somehow? Theo didn't think Pavel's scientific family would believe it even if they had. They thought all the stories Pavel had told them about Zmeykovo were just fairy tales.

"We'll get home sooner or later," Pavel said. "I believe in you. You're going to get rid of Lamia and Zlo soon enough."

Theo gulped down his emotion. It had been a while since he'd felt a part of the group.

Pavel continued, "Even if I don't get the Dracophone done before we go back home, I'll keep working on it. If you stay here … well, you'll need some way to keep in touch with me and your family."

"I …" Theo didn't know what to say. He had no clue what the future would hold.

Diva put her hands on both their shoulders. "After this is all over, it'll be easier to travel from Zmeykovo to Selo. Theo will be back and forth all the time. Won't you?"

Theo nodded.

"I like having you both here. When you go back, I'll really miss you." Diva's eyes twinkled. "I may need to come for a visit and see what you do for fun. I've always wanted to see the human world. Scare some more human boys the way I did you the first time."

Pavel blushed and put the schematic into his backpack. "Cool. I can take you to the mall to see all the neat stuff, or to a fair to get cotton candy, or even a movie or—"

"A date, Pavel?" Theo teased.

"No," Pavel hurriedly replied. "We'll all go together. You, me, Diva."

"What's a movie?" Diva asked. "You had talked about them once before, and they didn't sound much fun."

Theo laughed remembering Pavel spluttering on about scary movies after they'd seen a picture of the frightening Water Bull. "It's a book, but you don't read the words. You watch people act out the story."

Diva's eyes widened. "A live book?"

Theo and Pavel nodded. The three of them talked more, until Theo couldn't stay awake any longer. He grabbed a blanket and lay on the floor, wrapping his arms tight around his backpack to keep the Golden Apple safe. In the morning, he'd bring it back to the castle where it belonged. He drifted off into a deep, dreamless sleep, secure in his feelings about his friends for the first time in a while.

Chapter 14
Temple of a Goddess

JULY 11

LIGHT POURED INTO the room through a half-open door. Pavel and Magda were still resting, so Diva must have gone for her usual berries-and-herbs run. From outside, murmured voices of the coachmen showed no signs of distress. Theo was relieved the men had suffered no harm during the night. He himself had slept the sleep of the dead. He snorted, not intending to have used that word. Drakus would most certainly still be asleep. Hadn't he said he could only be active from noon to midnight?

One of the coachmen peered into the room. "Young Dragon Prince, the carriage has been restored, and we have received a message to bring you to the temple of the Great Goddess Bendis."

"What? Now?" Theo stretched and yawned. "What about my father? We have to go to the castle first to make sure he's okay."

"No need to worry about that." Magda rose from her blanket, not a trace of sleep in her eyes. "I'll return to take care of Zmey."

"Thank you." Theo turned to the coachmen. "We'll get ready, but we have to wait for Diva to return."

"You're going to have a long wait," Magda said. "Diva snuck out in the middle of the night, right after everyone else fell asleep."

Pavel stirred and rubbed his eyes. "She's probably patrolling. She looks for injured animals no matter where she is. She'll be back soon."

Magda shrugged. "Think what you want. I doubt she'll return this time. Last night, she was sneaking around to make sure everyone was asleep. She had something clutched close to her chest. It didn't look as if she was on an animal-rescue mission."

"I trust Diva." Theo meant it this time. If Diva truly had left, she had done so for a good reason. "Let's get packed up. We'll wait a little longer. We can always leave her a message here to let her know where we went."

Theo folded his blanket and replaced it by the bookshelf. He retrieved his sword and picked up his backpack. It felt lighter. He quickly opened it.

"No! It has to be here!" He scrambled around, looking at everything in the sparse room.

Pavel grabbed Theo's shoulders. "Hey, calm down. Whatever it is, we'll find it."

"No, you won't." Theo clutched his head in his hands as he paced. "The box with the Golden Apple is gone."

An I-told-you-so snicker came from Magda. "The apple's missing. Diva's missing. Hmm. Could there be a connection? I warned you that you couldn't trust her."

"No, no, no. I don't believe it!" Theo shouted at the same time Pavel said, "You did something to her."

"Drakus must have taken the apple," Theo said.

Pavel paled. "And kidnapped Diva."

"I can't believe I trusted a vampire, Oupir, or whatever he is. Kosara was right. Everyone wants the apple." Theo strapped on his backpack. "We'll track him down. Get Diva back. Get the apple."

"Theo, Theo," Magda said. "Your friend is right. You must calm down. Your anger will make you ill. Drakus never left his coffin. Diva is the only one missing."

"You're lying!" Theo stomped over and opened the casket lid. Drakus lay sound asleep.

Theo was numb. He felt like throwing up. Diva couldn't have taken the apple. Or if she had, it was to protect it. But why wouldn't she tell him? He really could use his mother's embrace right now.

Magda continued to talk, her voice soft, almost hypnotic, but Theo tuned her out. He didn't want to hear any more lies or accusations. He wasn't going to mistrust Diva again. In his heart, he knew she wouldn't betray him, no matter how dire the situation looked.

A thousand voices pierced Theo's mind, and a steady hum beat against his ears. He covered them, but the noises didn't stop. He crumpled to the floor. Magda's and Pavel's voices sounded distant, but Theo couldn't open his eyes to see them. He felt himself sinking into a cottony softness, wrapped in amber light. The voices faded, and all other sounds ceased. Trees appeared, trees cradling glowing orbs.

He'd returned to the Forest of Souls. He had to find Zunitza. She'd make everything better.

Her globe pulsed up ahead.

Theo ran to it. "Mom, I …"

It wasn't her in the globe. At least not her alone. Zmey had joined her.

Did he die while we were gone? Had Theo's decision to protect his friends resulted in his father's death? *Why does every choice I make hurt someone else?*

Mist filled the globe, blurring his parents' images. Theo's body lightened, and he felt himself twirling like a feather. Hundreds of fireflies darted around him as he traveled closer to the globe. They tried to nudge him inside, but he willed himself away. He wanted to be with Zunitza and Zmey, but Theo wasn't ready to die yet.

He blinked, and he was standing on the ground. The globe still glowed with an amber light in front of him. His mother appeared again. This time alone. Her mouth moved, but only choppy words reached him. "*Not your time. Go back. Protect the land. Save your father.*"

Zmey hadn't died. Theo breathed a sigh of relief. But if he was appearing in Zunitza's globe, he must be on the verge of death—more so than before.

Theo fought the trance. If that was what he was experiencing. He wanted to talk with his mother, but his father needed him.

Zunitza spoke again, but her words were even more broken and fading. "*Magda ... trust ... changed ... heart*" were all he could make out.

Did his mother want him to trust Magda? Zmey had said something similar when he was delirious. Or had he? But how could Theo trust Magda? She had such a dislike of Diva. And Theo vowed to himself he wouldn't doubt Diva's intentions again. His heart told him she would always be a friend.

That vision faded into mist, and another materialized. Eagles swarmed overhead, darkening the sky. They landed on the rock formations leading to the land of the giants and screeched. Theo's head throbbed, and tears flowed from his eyes from the unbearable pain. He covered his ears, but the sound continued to vibrate against his eardrums.

The uproar of the eagles faded, and another noise started as a low rumble. The rock formations began to crumble. Theo bolted as far away as he could and took cover within a cave as boulders the size of houses crashed around him. The land shuddered and cracked. Arms stretched forth from the rocky pillars, and legs followed. Voices like a nuclear explosion shattered what remained of the pillars.

The Ispolini had awoken!

That vision also faded, and the fireflies returned. They bumped into Theo's face, stinging him. He slapped at them, but they refused to leave. He'd never known them to bite before.

"Theo, can you hear me?" That voice wasn't his mother's.

Theo moaned and opened his eyes. Pavel's face was inches above his own.

"Oh, man, you scared me. You kept talking about giants and eagles. I'm glad you're finally awake." Pavel held a cup with a liquid to Theo's lips. "Drink this. Magda said it would make you feel better."

Theo took small sips of the herbal concoction. It tasted minty, unlike most of the foul drinks Baba Yaga had made him drink when he'd needed healing. His energy revived, and he sat up. Someone had wrapped warm blankets around him. He was in the carriage, but it was traveling along the ground, instead of flying. And he and Pavel were alone.

"Where's Magda? Did Diva come back?"

"Magda returned to the castle." Pavel looked down. "No, Diva didn't come back. But I know she didn't steal the apple."

"I agree. She's not a thief. Something else happened." Theo rubbed his temple. The pain was receding. "What happened to me? My head felt as if it were full of lead."

Pavel handed Theo the rest of the drink. "Take this. Magda said it was some kind of poisoning, from black magic. She thinks Sirin's song left a mark on you."

Theo pursed his lips. He wasn't sure that was the cause of his collapse. Sirin's song hadn't left any trace of evil in him. Her intent wasn't to do harm, but to bring joy and peace—even though that ended up being achieved through death. It wasn't the bird's fault. The curse turned her gift into a destructive force.

"We have to get back to the castle. I need to make sure Zmey is okay. Then we need to find out what happened to Diva."

"No can do right now," Pavel said. "I wish we could, but the coachmen said they're under strict orders to get you to Bendis' temple first."

A thought niggled in the back of Theo's mind. He tried to recall something Kosara had said about Bendis when they'd taken refuge at the Znahar Tree to protect themselves against Lamia and her hoard. He snapped his fingers. She'd said Bendis couldn't return until the menace of Lamia and Zlo had been removed and order restored to Zmeykovo. What was so important that she had returned now? Or had the coachmen received a false message, and all of them were heading into a trap?

The carriage bumped over rocky ground. Theo looked out the window. "Why aren't we flying?"

"Magda said the altitude would harm you and told the coachmen not to fly."

Magda said this. Magda said that. His aunt was making a lot of decisions. Theo held on tight as the carriage rattled down the path. He hoped it was actually taking them to the temple.

THEO BREATHED A SIGH of relief when a massive pure white tree appeared. They had arrived at the temple, and nothing had attacked them along the way.

On his first trip to Zmeykovo, Diva had told him that Bendis had planted the tree when the temple had been completed. The trunk was so large that the building had to have been completed thousands of years ago. Unfortunately, on that day, he and Diva had discovered that the temple had been burned to the ground, and Bendis had fled. Now she was back, but it still wasn't safe. Whatever it was she wanted to see Theo about had to be extremely important for her to dare to venture back.

The tree marked the entrance to a tunnel that led to the temple. Branches of trees on both sides of a path had intertwined with those of the ancient white tree's massive limbs to form the tunnel. It created a secure entrance to the temple, at least from the ground.

When they reached the end of the tunnel, Theo was glad to see that the temple had been rebuilt. He hoped that they hadn't done this too soon, with Lamia and Zlo still rampaging the land. Perhaps they'd put in some kind of security system. The last time,

Lamia had struck without warning. At least now, they knew the terrors existed and could prepare for an attack.

The carriage stopped in front of a white marble building surrounded by mist. The temple reminded Theo of a pagoda, but it contained elements of other temples he'd seen pictures of. It had a dome with a spire and columns surrounding an open porch-like area. A white marble path led to a massive wooden door, surrounded by two columns.

A carved spiral of the sun adorned the center of the door, with jewel-encrusted rays extending toward the edges. Mounted on top of each of the columns on either side of the door was a golden winged creature. Its head was that of a horse, its body a lizard, and a long snake tail wound around the sides.

Two golden-haired women, clothed in dark green tunics and leather boots decorated with fox fur, guarded the doorway. They held their spears crossed, barring entrance to the temple.

"Wow, it's amazing!" Pavel gaped at the building. "How are we going to get in? Those guards don't look friendly."

"All will be well." One of the coachmen ascended the marble steps, bowed to the women, and presented them a gold token emblazoned with the image of the Firebird and Znahar Tree.

The guards uncrossed their spears and opened the doors.

The coachman waved Theo and Pavel forward. "This way, Young Dragon Prince and guest."

They walked down a long, drafty corridor lined with marble columns and mosaics decorating the floor. Amber light from oil lamps illuminated murals lining the walls. Theo shivered from the cold and the image of a three-headed monster attacking women with bows. Dressed like the guards, the women in the mural hurled javelins at the dragon, which had to be Lamia, while they rode flying carriages drawn by winged deer. More murals lined the walls, but he didn't have time to view them all. He didn't want to keep Bendis waiting.

The corridor ended at an ornate door, decorated with a jeweled representation of the Firebird. A guard at the door opened it when the coachman presented the golden token.

Inside, a pool with sparkling sapphire water lay before the goddess' golden throne. Covered with white pelts, the throne rose high above them. On the far wall, ceiling-to-floor turquoise curtains bordered a massive door carved with three moons. Two women dressed like the ones at the entrance stood guard by it.

Pavel gulped. "How tall is Diva's goddess?"

Theo had wondered the same thing.

The guards opened the doors, and light filled the room as the goddess entered.

An athletic woman glided toward the throne. She was tall, but not the giant Theo had expected. She wore a mask of falcon feathers and a long, white robe embroidered in gold with symbols of the sun, moon, Firebird, and many others Theo didn't recognize. The bottom of her garment swept across the marble tiles. Tattoos similar to Diva's decorated her exposed arms. More than that, golden serpents coiled around each arm from her shoulder to her wrist.

Two black dogs, each the size of a horse, lunged forward to escort her to the throne. Snarling, they crouched on either side of the goddess as she sat.

A woman bowed before the goddess and held out a tray with grapes and a golden rhyton filled with wine. Bendis raised the drink to her lips.

Theo and Pavel approached the throne, and both kneeled on the marble floor.

"Please stand." Bendis signaled with her hand. "I have called you here to assist you with the battle ahead. You have light within you, and this will aid you in your journey to destroy the darkness."

Light within me ... This was the third time Theo had heard those words. He recalled what both the statue and his father had said: *He who has light within himself will tear apart the darkness.* He waited for Bendis to say more, and he hoped she would explain the meaning of the words.

The goddess continued, "I cannot directly interfere in your affairs, but I can give you a gift. How you use it is up to you, but I know you won't disappoint me and your people. Come forward and hold out your sword."

Theo bowed and approached the throne. He unsheathed his sword and pointed the tip to the floor. The dogs beside the goddess growled.

Bendis laid a hand on each of their heads. "You must point it toward me to receive your gift. Fear not, my beasts will not harm you."

With shaking hands, Theo lifted his sword.

Bendis rose. Touching the sun on her garment, she said, "Tangra has found you worthy." Next, she touched the moon. "And I, too, have found you worthy." Finally, she touched the Firebird. "Our priestess Kosara has found you worthy." Each time the goddess touched a symbol on her robe, the item glowed: white for Tangra, blue for Bendis, and red for the Firebird.

With all three images burning bright, Bendis raised her arms above her head. "Tangra gives his blessing to you, the rays of the sun. I bestow upon you the cyclical power of the moon, to draw forward or to push away. And Kosara grants you the ability to harness the fire of the Firebird."

First, her fingers glowed, then her hands, and with her last words, the goddess' entire arms shone with swirling colors that combined into a violet hue. Bendis lowered her arms and pointed them toward the sword that Theo held. He latched on with both hands to keep it steady.

A blast of light shot like lightning from the goddess' fingertips and struck the tip of the sword. The weapon blazed. The light traveled up to the hilt. Theo's fingers tingled at the touch. The light crept along his hands, up his arms, past his shoulders, and over the rest of his body until Theo shone like a shooting star.

Energy unlike any he'd ever felt before filled his body, mind, and soul. His dragon spirit roared. Visions passed in front of Theo's eyes so rapidly he couldn't tell where one ended and another began. He saw the realm of the gods. From afar, he looked down upon the Earth. And he experienced the rebirth of the Firebird.

When the light faded, Theo found himself prone on the floor, the sword still clutched in his hands. He raised himself to discover the symbols from Bendis' robe—the sun, moon, and Firebird— were now etched upon the sword's hilt. He looked up to thank the goddess, but she had disappeared.

Chapter 15
Where Is Diva?

BACK AT THE CASTLE, Theo wandered around the rose garden. Ula had greeted him, telling him his father's condition hadn't worsened, but he remained delirious, and it was best to let Magda attend to him. Theo had agreed, not wanting to be in his aunt's presence. Her continued insistence that Diva was some kind of evil monster irritated him. He had to discover what had happened to his friend, if she truly had taken the Golden Apple. And if so, then why. He had wanted to ask Bendis, but she had disappeared before he had a chance. Now, only one person might be able to give him that information. Jabalaka Theo used his dragon senses to make sure no one was observing him, and then he scrambled under the gazebo to make his way to the hidden library.

At the end of the tunnel, Theo inserted a token into a slot in the wooden door. Jabalaka had set up the security system to ensure no one except Sly could enter the library from that passageway. At least until Theo showed up. Then Jabalaka explained how to return to the library if he needed help, but to use it sparingly, for fear of someone discovering Jabalaka was alive.

Theo believed finding Diva was a justifiable reason to return.

As the door creaked open, Sly's voice drifted out. "Master, where I leave these books?"

The Vodnik's webbed feet appeared under a pile of swaying books that looked as if they were ready to topple.

"By the table is fine," Jabalaka replied.

Theo went over as Sly reached his destination and grabbed a couple of books about to slide from the top. "Here you go." Theo held out the books to the Vodnik.

"My King, my King! Sly is so happy to see you!"

The books tumbled to the floor as Sly rushed to bow his head.

"Stop. Sly, stop. I'm not a king!"

"Theo?" Jabalaka poked his head around the door to the smaller library room. "Why are you here? Is everything okay?"

"No." Theo shook his head. "Diva's gone missing, and we need to find her."

"Tell me what happened." Jabalaka came into the room. The man still had a bit of a waddle from the time he had to walk around on frog-like webbed feet. He sat on a chair and swiped back his tuft of hair.

Theo paced as he explained everything that had happened since he'd left the library. "And now Diva's gone. The Golden Apple's gone. And Magda keeps pushing the idea that Diva stole it and wants the power for herself."

Jabalaka shook his head. "Oh, oh, oh. Anyone who loves books the way that Samodiva does cannot be a bad apple." He chuckled at his joke.

Theo groaned. This wasn't the time for bad puns. "I was hoping you knew of a way to find where she is."

"Yes, yes." Jabalaka grunted as he got up from the chair.

Theo wondered why older people always did that. They could sit down without groaning, but they couldn't seem to get up without the noise.

"Let me see." He looked around the room, still swimming in stacks of books. "Sly, do you recall where I put my special tools?"

"Oh, yes, Master. I go get them." Sly hopped away to a far corner of the room, dug through piles of books, and came back dragging a bulging satchel.

"Thank you, my friend." Jabalaka took the bag and dumped its contents onto the floor.

An assortment of items flew out: a copper bowl, wooden tiles, string, bells, candles, incense, vials with sloshing liquids, and more curiosities hidden beneath the pile.

Jabalaka rubbed his chin. "Hmm, what would be best in this situation?"

"Do the words. Do the words." Sly hopped around picking up tiles that had scattered under a table.

"The runic tiles?" Jabalaka shrugged. "A good choice."

As Sly picked through the objects to gather all the tiles, Theo recognized symbols on them. Some of them were the same as the ones on his medallion. The ancient writing of Zmeykovo. Theo rubbed his chest. A faint outline of the words "Unborn Hero" was still etched where the medallion had seared his skin.

Sly dumped the tiles onto the table next to Jabalaka. It looked as if the two of them were getting ready for a game of Scrabble, but with only nine tiles.

As Jabalaka picked up the runes, he chanted, "Oh, Thracian gods of old, we seek your divine guidance. We beseech you to answer the question set before you. What has become of our good Samodiva friend? Has any trouble befallen her?"

He tossed the tiles onto the table. Some landed with the rune exposed, while others appeared face down. Jabalaka examined the symbols, running his fingertips over their surface, once more chanting, "Oh, Thracian gods of old, grant me a vision of our missing friend."

With his eyes closed, Jabalaka repeated his request, the words becoming softer with each iteration, until only his lips moved.

"Oh, oh, oh." Jabalaka tore his hands away from the tiles. "No, it can't be true."

"What is it?" Theo peered at the tiles, seeing nothing but the symbols. "What did you see?"

"I must try again, another way." Jabalaka picked up the copper bowl. "Sly—"

Theo grabbed Jabalaka's shoulders. "What did they tell you? I need to know."

Jabalaka's eyes bugged out. "I heard a whisper about the land of the Ispolini."

"The giants. Diva's in the land of the giants?" Theo stepped back. His mouth went dry. "That doesn't mean she's at …" He let the words trail off. The Ispolini had lived in the land on the other side of Cherna Mountain, where Zmey's castle stood. She could be anywhere there, hiding, to protect the Golden Apple, if indeed she even had it.

"Let me try another way, that will paint me a picture." Jabalaka held the copper bowl out to Sly. "Dear friend, will you fill this with water? Not to the top, mind you. Halfway will be enough."

"Yes, yes, Master." Sly took the bowl and hopped away.

"Doesn't it bother you that he still calls you master?" Theo asked. "You're not their leader in the swamp any longer."

Jabalaka shook his head. "I never was their master there either. Sly and the other Vodni took it upon themselves to give me that title after I … Well, I saved many of them some hardships."

"I wish he would stop calling me a king." Theo ran his fingers through his hair. "My father is the king."

Jabalaka let out a long breath. "You will never convince him to call you anything else. Once Sly begins to idolize anyone, there is no changing his mind. He may be an uncomplicated being, but he is devoted. Accept the honor he has bestowed upon you."

"I guess." Theo shrugged. All this royalty stuff still made him feel uneasy. Not long ago, he was able to just be a human boy from Selo, with his greatest worry being whether or not he could catch enough fish for his family.

Sly bounded back. Water sloshed over the edges of the bowl. He set it down on the table. Jabalaka picked through the items on the floor and selected a flat, shiny stone. With it in his palm, he held his hand over the water and repeated his earlier chant to the Thracian gods of old. Then, he dropped the stone into the water. It rippled, and the stone gave off an iridescent glow.

With his nose almost touching the edge of the bowl, Jabalaka stared into the water. "A picture's forming."

Theo looked, too, but he saw only the stone lying at the bottom.

"I see Diva clutching onto Sur as he speeds through the sky. They race toward a mountain."

Theo held his breath. Had Diva come to the castle? Was she hiding here all along? What had made her flee from the demon forest? She wasn't afraid of anything as far as Theo knew.

"A structure is forming in the distance," Jabalaka continued. "The castle." He paused. "No, they're flying past. Into more rocky terrain. Towers. A fortress. She's at the gate." Jabalaka lifted his head. His voice squeaked as he said, "She entered Kaleto Fortress. Guards welcomed her."

"I don't believe it!" Theo swiped the bowl from the table. Water flew through the air, and the stone clattered against the floor. "Try something else. Don't you have a crystal ball?"

"These are my best resources for this type of divination." Jabalaka patted away water that had spilled onto his lap. "It's true that it's been a while since I've used them. Something could be wrong. Like fine-tuning a piano, they may need to be purified."

"What about the apple? Did you see her with the Golden Apple?" Theo asked.

Jabalaka sighed. "I can try again, asking that question."

Sly didn't have to be asked. He gathered the bowl and stone and hopped away to get more water. The Vodnik placed the items onto the table and scurried away.

Jabalaka repeated his ritual, this time asking the gods if Diva had the Golden Apple with her. When he received his answer, Jabalaka squeezed his hands together and nodded.

Theo clenched his teeth, thanked Jabalaka, and stormed out of the library. Back in the rose garden, he paced the paths. *Something has to be wrong. Diva wouldn't willingly fly to Kaleto.*

Sur! Theo stopped pacing. Jabalaka said Diva had flown to Kaleto on her deer. *I can ask Sur what really happened.* Diva's deer companion was her best friend. The two of them had a special bond, the way all deer and their companions did. The two could talk with one another with their minds. They sensed each other's emotions and if they were in danger.

He rushed to the field where the deer grazed. When he found Sur, Theo strode over to the animal. "Sur, I need to know where Diva is. Please help me."

Sur's globe turned light purple. He snorted and pawed the dirt.

"I don't know what that means." Theo placed his hand on Sur's side and mentally repeated the words.

The deer backed away, the orb turning a darker purple with sparks flying from it.

"*Shar*," Theo thought to his own deer companion, "*can you help me? I need to talk with Sur.*"

Theo's companion came flying over and rubbed his head against Theo. The two deer snorted at each other for a while. Sur grew increasingly agitated, tossing his head and hurling dirt behind him as he dug deeper into the soil.

Shar nuzzled Theo again. "*Sur says he will not betray Diva. She has forbidden him from saying anything.*"

This didn't sound good. Even so, Theo didn't want to believe the worst of Diva again. "Please, Sur, if she's at Kaleto—"

Sur backed away, even more sparks flying off of his orb.

"I think she's in danger," Theo continued. "I'm sure you don't want Diva harmed."

Sur's orb danced with flashes of purple, then amber, as if he couldn't make up his mind about whether to help Theo or not. The deer let out a grunt as he tossed his head from side to side. All six wings stretched and flapped.

Theo looked from Sur to his deer. *"Shar, what's he saying? Is there any way he can talk with me the way you and I do?"*

Once more the deer communicated with each other.

"Put your hand on my side and the other on Sur's," Shar spoke to Theo's mind. *"He says he can only* show *you something. You will have to decide for yourself what it means."*

Theo did as Sur requested. An image appeared in his mind. Diva walking toward the fortress gates, the box containing the Golden Apple tucked tight to her chest. She looked straight ahead, and her gaze was dead, her eyes black. She stepped inside the fortress without a backward glance or a goodbye to Sur.

Chapter 16
Unexpected Visit

BACK AT THE GAZEBO, Theo sat with his head cradled in his hands as his mind tried to unravel what Sur had shown him. Had Diva been drugged? Or, in Zmeykovo, it was more likely that magic had been used against her—black magic.

Who had the opportunity to do that? Diva was always alert to the dangers around her. She had been captured before, but Theo had never seen her so out of it. It was as if she were a ghost of herself. A zombie.

He laid out the possibilities in his mind.

His first suspect was Magda. His aunt had tried so hard to convince Theo of Diva's guilt. He still couldn't figure out why. What did Magda expect to gain from making Diva look bad? And when did she have the opportunity to put a spell on Diva?

Theo thought back to the day before. He had gone to sleep before the others. Diva and Pavel were inside, and Magda was outside. Theo had no idea what had occurred after he fell asleep, and he hadn't heard a thing during the night. Even in her sleep, though, Diva was aware of what was happening. So, how was it possible that Magda—or anyone, in fact—had been able to get to Diva?

Drakus was another possibility. But his curse prevented him from being active during the time Diva disappeared. Had he done something to Diva beforehand? It was possible the Oupir worked with Sirin. Drakus could have asked Sirin to implant some hidden message into Diva's mind when the bird was singing. After all, Drakus did say that Sirin was once his beloved. But, again, why would they do that?

The coachmen? No. Theo dismissed them. But how had Diva gotten past them? The men were taking turns repairing the carriage and being on guard. Theo doubted the men slept at all that night, especially not all of them. And it was unlikely that they allowed a demon from the forest to get past them to abduct Diva.

Why didn't someone think to ask the coachmen if they'd seen Diva? Theo didn't have the chance, since he'd passed out.

The only one left was Pavel, and Theo immediately crossed his friend off the list. There was no way Pavel would do anything harmful to Diva.

"Ahhhh." Theo stood and paced the gazebo. "I'm not going to figure this out until I know what motivated someone to enchant Diva."

He needed his friends to help him figure this out. If Diva had brought the Golden Apple to Kaleto Fortress, it was likely Lamia now had the fruit. Theo and his friends had to find a way to get both the apple and Diva back, without harming her.

First, he wanted to check to see how his father was doing. The day was almost over, and Theo hadn't seen Zmey yet.

As he made his way down the path, lights shimmered by the rose bush his mother had planted. Someone was there. And the person was dancing. *How odd. Who is it?*

Theo hurried toward the terrace, but stopped before he reached it. It was a woman, wearing a dress covered with gold coins. A white veil covered her face. *Is that my mother's wedding dress?*

Anger bubbled to the surface, so strong it roused Theo's dragon spirit. *Who dares disrespect my mother, Zmeykovo's queen, by wearing her wedding gown?*

Theo stormed toward the woman. "What do you think you're doing?"

The woman stopped dancing. Slowly, she turned to face him and lifted the veil.

Magda!

"Why are you wearing my mother's wedding dress?" he yelled.

She had accused Diva of stealing Zunitza's belt, yet now Magda herself was taking something of his mother's.

His aunt cowered and stepped back, her eyes wide and her mouth gaping. "I … I'm sorry. I just became overwhelmed with missing my sister, and I wanted to feel close to her. I cherish my memories of her, but that wasn't enough. I didn't mean any harm."

"After thirteen years?" Theo shook his head in disbelief. He had been taught to respect his elders, especially family members, but his aunt was behaving badly. Why all of a sudden was she *missing* her sister? Magda hadn't shown any remorse or nostalgia about Zunitza before now. And besides that …

He took a deep breath, letting it escape slowly. "Shouldn't you be with my father, instead of dancing in my mother's dress?"

Magda lowered her head. "I needed a break. Ula's with Zmey."

"Fine." Theo waved toward the castle. "Maybe you should go back and let me cool off."

Magda looked around, and then took a step back. She gasped. "Who's that? No one should be out here."

A girl with red braids approached from one of the paths. She carried a basket of apples.

"Who are you? I haven't seen you here before," Theo said. "And why are you in the garden?"

"I came to the castle earlier today. I rushed here as fast as I could." She bowed her head and spoke in a soft voice. "I was out picking apples when my village was attacked."

"Lamia!" Theo growled. "I have to get others to go help."

"Your guards have already sent people there," the girl replied.

"What are you doing out here?" Theo said with a gruff voice. He still fumed at Magda. "You shouldn't be wandering around the castle grounds." He turned to his aunt. "Magda, take her inside and find someone to watch her."

The girl's eyes darkened, and her face contorted with malice. "Don't tell me what to do!"

She gritted her teeth as she smashed the basket of apples to the ground. The girl began to convulse. Theo thought she was about to explode as her body swelled. It grew and grew, forming a snake tail, covered with golden scales that were streaked with black. The red hair became golden, and this too had black strands throughout.

Lamia stared back at Theo with her dark reptilian eyes.

Golden scales covered the sleeves of her garment like armor. What looked like a red scarf made of sharp, pointed knife tips encircled the bodice.

Her gaze shot past Theo to Magda. Sneering, Lamia hissed. "You're so pathetic. Always trying to become your sister. Do you want to end up like her as well—lying in a coffin with unseeing eyes?"

Magda trembled and hid behind Theo.

He spread out his arms to block Lamia's advance. Magda had annoyed him, but that didn't mean he wanted Lamia to hurt his other aunt. "Don't touch her. This is between you and me."

"So true. Be gone!" Lamia roared to Magda. "I have a private matter to discuss with my *dear nephew*."

Magda scurried away like a frightened mouse. Her feet clattered against the tiles, racing like Theo's heart. He had wanted Lamia here, so he and his friends could trap her. But now, it was only him and her. Because he had been summoned to harvest the apple, he hadn't had the time to set the trap. His aunt wore the ouroboros belt, stroking the white dragon that was swallowing its tail, as if she were taunting Theo that it belonged to his father.

He looked toward the balcony, where they had planned to capture her.

"That wouldn't have worked," Lamia said.

"What?"

"Your naïve plan. How foolish do you think I am to fall for something like that?"

Theo sighed. He should have known Lamia would have found out about their plan. It was doomed to fail even before they started.

Maybe I can still get the belt from her by myself. He inched his hand closer to his sword.

Lamia flicked her fingers toward Theo, and his body froze. "Not nice, *dear nephew*. I didn't come here to fight."

"I didn't invite you to a party, either," he shot back. "What do you want? I have important matters to deal with."

"A party?" Lamia laughed. "Surprising you'd say that. You may not have invited me to one, but I'm here to give you an invitation to a ball. I shall soon become the queen of Zmeykovo when I consume the Golden Apple that your Samodiva friend so willingly brought to me."

"You lie!" Theo struggled to move, but remained stuck in his frozen position. "You always lie. I saw how she'd been put under a spell."

"Has she now?" Lamia slithered nearer, running her clawed fingers down Theo's cheek. "She's been enjoying the life of a princess in Kaleto."

"Like my sister, Nia, did?" Theo shot back. "You gave her everything she thought she wanted, but you were going to sacrifice Nia in the end."

"Power does require sacrifices."

Sparks ignited in Lamia's eyes. To Theo, they seemed to harbor some deep-hidden anger. What kind of sacrifice did Lamia have to make to get where she was now? Regardless of any pain she'd suffered, she had no right to demand others to sacrifice for her gain.

"Why would I want to witness you becoming even more evil?"

"Evil?" Lamia curled her tail around the marble pedestal on the terrace and hurled it among the roses, uprooting the bush Zunitza had planted. "You don't know what true evil is. You've never been under Zlo's thrall."

"Yes, I have." Theo snarled back at her, even though his insides shook remembering the event.

Zlo had slipped inside Theo's mind, hypnotizing him into believing he was useless. The monster had told Theo he was no leader. That he was only an unimportant little boy. Zlo's voice had penetrated deep into Theo's subconsciousness, attempting to force him to be stuck there forever, remembering all his failures.

Lamia whispered into his ear, "Then you'll understand why I need your help defeating Zlo."

"I told you before that I'd never help you."

"And I also told you there's a secret that will tear you apart."

"I don't believe you. If you really wanted to defeat Zlo," Theo said, "you'd return my father's belt. The two of you together would be powerful."

Lamia spun away. Her eyes hardened. "I'll never seek Zmey's help. I cannot … My brother is better off dead, since he's dying to be with his *beloved Samodiva*." She spit out the last two words like a curse, before she slithered closer to Theo again. "But we could accomplish all the things my brother and I never could."

"I want nothing to do with you." What Theo wanted was to tear Lamia apart. Siblings shouldn't hate one another the way Lamia did Zmey. "I don't need your help to defeat Zlo. I have real friends who will stand by my side. You have no one, and by yourself, you're … *nothing*."

"I am not nothing!" She screeched and scales erupted all over her body. "With everything I have suffered, I deserve the Golden Apple! If you're wise, you'll become my ally. I might even let your father live."

"I'll save him without your help."

"You won't be able to stop me." She scratched her claws down his face again, just short of drawing blood. "I expect to see you at the ball, dressed appropriately and not smelling or looking like a peasant. If you don't appear, your poor Samodiva friend will die."

"You've tried before and failed at that, too," Theo said.

"Success will be mine this time." Lamia dropped at Theo's feet an envelope engraved with a golden swooping L and a crest with a three-headed dragon. "We're family. I want you to be part of this momentous occasion."

Theo glared at her. "Family means nothing to you. Look at how you treat your brother, your own twin."

"Yes, one day ask your father about family loyalty. If he survives, that is." Lamia laughed as her body grew larger, and scales covered her skin. "And I forgot to mention. Come alone. The invitation is for one only. Let your friends stay at the castle so they can babysit your father."

Lamia's eyes darkened, and her teeth grew larger, with sharp tips. Her face elongated into dragon form, and two more burst from her body. Six fierce eyes stared at him as she hissed. With a roar, she leapt into the darkening sky. A flock of small green dragons flew out of the trees and joined her as she zoomed away, back to Kaleto Fortress.

The sky cracked open with lightning, and thunder boomed. Sheets of ice battered the ground, covering Zunitza's uprooted roses.

Theo's paralysis left him, and he clenched his sword. When he encountered Lamia again, he'd be better prepared to fight her. Now, it was time to gather the troops. Theo might have to go to the ball as a princely attendee in order to ensure Diva's safety, but he most certainly wouldn't go alone.

Chapter 17
Battle Plans

THEO FELT THE WEIGHT of everyone's despair. The number of those meeting in Zmey's den had dwindled from when they'd first set out to defeat Lamia and Zlo. Without Diva, the group had lost its vibrancy. Now, only Sava and Ula represented the Samodivi.

Jega sat with his head clenched within his palms. He'd lost two brothers in this war. Zima had perished, and Mraz was in hiding, keeping the secrets in *Lamia's Bible* safe from being exploited.

And Pavel. Exhaustion and pain reflected on his face. Theo could tell Pavel was missing Diva and still held a trace of guilt over Zima's death, although Sirin had eradicated most of it with her song.

Sitara hadn't been able to make it, but Jega had assured everyone that he would inform the blacksmith of their plans. Magda and Drakus were also missing, not that Theo would have invited them. He didn't know how to contact Drakus, anyway, without returning to the demon forest—which he had no plans to do. Drakus had said he'd be able to find Theo when it was time to battle Lamia. That, in itself, was troubling.

Too many questions remained unanswered about both Magda's and Drakus' motivations or loyalty. After her reaction to Lamia out on the terrace, Theo had second thoughts about Magda's guilt concerning Diva's disappearance. If his aunt was so terrified, would she be in league with Lamia to destroy Zmeykovo? Even if Magda wasn't his enemy, he didn't fully trust her.

Drakus had now become his number one suspect, although Theo wasn't certain the Oupir was the real culprit. He lacked any motivation to befriend Lamia. The opposite was true instead. The man hated her with a passion. What was that popular saying? Keep your friends close and your enemies closer. If Drakus was their enemy, Theo wanted to keep an eye on him.

Anyway, it was time to make plans with his friends who were present. Theo cleared his throat, and everyone looked his way. "I have good news and bad news."

Pavel groaned. "At least there's good news."

"I know a way into Kaleto." He held up the invitation. "I've been invited to a ball tomorrow night."

"A ball?" Pavel's voice rose. "This isn't the time to go dancing."

"The only kind of dancing I plan to do is with my sword." Theo glanced around the room. The others looked at him with hope in their eyes, although they remained silent. "It won't so much be dancing, anyway. Lamia said—"

Pavel paled. "Lamia gave you the invitation? She was here? And that's the good news?"

"Yes, it was from her." Theo explained how his aunt had tricked the guards and him, too. And how she had claimed she wanted him to help her against Zlo. Even more important, Theo told them that Lamia would kill Diva if he didn't attend. "It's good news because I'll have an excuse to be there before she eats the apple. I'll have a chance to save Diva, get Zmey's belt, and stop the ceremony."

"It sounds like a trick, Theo," Sava said. "What's the bad news?"

"Lamia told me to come alone."

The previously subdued room exploded with objections.

Theo waved his hands, gesturing for everyone to become quiet. "No, I hadn't planned to go alone. I can enter through the main gate, but we need to figure out a way for everyone else to get inside."

"Diva has a book of maps that Sly gave her for her birthday," Pavel said. "I'll go get it." He rushed away without waiting for anyone to respond.

The book had been one of Jabalaka's that Sly had in his possession. The Vodnik had been present when Theo, Pavel, and Diva had discovered that Jabalaka's home in the Cold Marsh had been destroyed and his books burned. Sly had seen Diva's frantic behavior and had rightly thought that a book would be the best present he could give her.

"The book is a great idea," Sava said. "We cannot enter Kaleto the way the Samodivi did last time. When we exited the tunnel into the fortress courtyard, we met with resistance. It's certain that the passageway will be either heavily fortified or impassible now."

Theo turned to Jega. "Do you know of any way the Kukeri have entered the fortress in the past?"

Jega shook his head. "We have had no need to do so during my lifetime. The only way in I know of is the way we entered before, and that was Zima's…" Jega's face crumpled. "My muse is gone. My friend, my brother. The light has gone from my soul."

Ula wrapped an arm around Jega's waist. "We'd understand if you decide you cannot accompany us on this mission."

Jega's eyes hardened. "I am ready and capable of fighting. I will not let that beast win."

Pavel ran into the room, breathless. "Here's the book. I—"

His words were interrupted by the flapping of wings. A colony of bats entered the den. The funnel of black creatures swirled and transformed into Drakus.

"Wow, what an entrance," Pavel said.

Drakus bowed his head to everyone but remained silent.

Pavel handed Theo the book. "A page that looked like it was an entrance to Kaleto was already marked."

"May I see?" Sava came over and examined the map. "As I feared, this is the entrance we used previously. We'll have to find another way."

"Perhaps I can be of assistance," Drakus said. "I know of several ways directly inside the fortress itself, rather than into the courtyard, where many other passageways lead. May I see the book to determine if they're included?"

Theo nodded and gave Drakus the book. "We'll need to get as close as possible to the ballroom. That's where I assume the ceremony will take place, the same place Zlo performed the ritual to bring back Lamia."

Drakus sat at the desk, flipping through the book, stopping to examine some maps more closely. He tore off pieces of parchment that littered the desk and marked pages with them. The room remained quiet, except for the crinkling of paper and everyone's breaths.

An hour or so passed before Drakus stood and stretched his shoulders. "I think I have the best solution. If you all would gather around, I'll explain my plan."

Theo and Pavel stood on either side of Drakus, while Sava, Ula, and Jega looked over the Oupir's shoulders.

Drakus flipped to the first marked page and pointed. "There's an outcropping of rocks not far from the fortress. It leads into a drainage closet."

"What kind of drainage?" Theo remembered trudging through muck to get into Zmey's castle on his first trip to Zmeykovo. From Pavel's scrunched up face, he was remembering that, too.

"The tunnel was dug so underwater channels could be cleaned and repaired when necessary," Drakus replied.

Pavel grumbled, "I'm not walking through another cesspool or sewer. That sounds like it would be full of rats and filth."

"It's nothing as offensive as that." Drakus turned a few pages. "This tunnel here drains the dirty water from the kitchen and bathroom facilities. It also brings you into the fortress, but not close enough to the ballroom. The water that's in the tunnel I'm suggesting comes from mineral pools and is used for drinking. It's pumped up into the fortress through huge pipes."

"Thank heavens." Pavel wiped his brow. "If they have mineral pools, they should upgrade and build a spa. They could make good money by being an all-inclusive resort. I wonder if we could—"

Theo nudged Pavel. "We need to focus on getting into the fortress, not on opening spas." To Drakus, Theo said, "Where does your suggested route lead? Do you have a floor plan?"

"Let me show you." Drakus turned to another page. "This is an old plan, but it's unlikely the structure has changed. A now-unused section of the pipes comes up here." He pointed to a room. "It's a closet within a bathroom. Another door inside the closet hides the pipe. The top is exposed, so everyone should be able to exit when they reach the end. From the bathroom, you go down this passageway, which leads to the main corridor. And the ballroom is here, right off to the side." He traced the way as he spoke.

"That seems easy enough," Theo said. "Once everyone is inside, you can all come to the ballroom. I'll try to prevent anything from happening before you arrive."

"There's a problem, actually more than one," Drakus added. "That closet is locked, so you'll have to find a way to get there and unlock it for everyone. Jega could break the door down, but that would alert patrols to our presence."

Theo examined the map. "There are a lot of passageways from the main entry up to this point. How am I supposed to know which one to take?"

"There used to be a picture of the Ispolini building the fortress right here before you get there." Drakus pointed. "I can't imagine anyone would have moved it. Lamia didn't seem like the kind to redecorate."

Theo stared at the layout again, counting the numerous corridors as a safeguard, in case the situation had changed. He figured he'd be so nervous that he might actually need to make that pit stop. "What are the other problems?"

"The tunnels have many turnoffs, and there are places where you'll be completely submerged in water."

"I guess that means the rest of us don't get to wear party clothes," Pavel said.

Theo rolled his eyes, ignoring his friend. "We can get Rusalki belts, so breathing shouldn't be a problem. And no one should get lost if you're showing them the way."

"Unfortunately, I cannot lead you." Drakus shook his head. "As a demon, I'm unable to cross water. But you'll find scratch marks pointing out the way you should go."

"How will you get in, then?" Theo asked.

"I can fly down a chimney. I'll meet you all at the ballroom."

"I guess we have a plan. I'll go in the main gate, Drakus will come down the chimney, and the rest of you will use the tunnel. Is everyone okay with that?" Theo locked around the room as his friends nodded.

However, he sensed a trap. Once Drakus left, the rest of them would look through the book again to see if they could find another method for getting inside. Either way, Theo planned to ask Jega to keep an eye on Drakus once they were in the fortress. Theo's dragon senses tingled. He was certain something was going to go wrong.

Chapter 18
The Prince Arrives

JULY 12

THE NEXT EVENING after Sitara arrived, everyone went over the plans again. The blacksmith had forged new spears and arrow tips for the warriors, and he gave Pavel a dagger. All that remained was for Theo to dress like a prince. This was the worst part. The fighting Theo could handle, but he felt prissy having to wear what he thought would be some fancy costume.

"It won't be so bad," Ula told him. "You'll see. Come with me so you can get ready."

She led him past his father's room. Theo had stopped by earlier in the day, but his father remained unresponsive. Tonight would see the end of Zmey's suffering. Theo was determined to return with the ouroboros belt. Magda had eventually shooed Theo away, saying his presence agitated his father, and the man needed to rest.

Ula stopped at the next door and opened it to reveal a dressing room lit by torches. A plump maid wearing a green puff dress bowed to him as he entered. Her white hair was done up in a bun, with escaped strands curled around her ears.

"*Tsk, tsk*," she said as she circled him. "This is no manner of dress for a future ruler. A prince must look like one. How can you prove yourself, looking like a rascal?"

The maid disappeared into the back of a closet filled with shelves of jackets, pants, shirts, shoes, and belts. A clatter of falling boxes came from within, followed by a groan.

Theo rushed to the closet door. "Are you okay?"

"Yes," her muffled response came.

Shuffling and dragging of boxes, followed by the clacking of the maid's shoes had Theo wondering how big the closet was and how much clothing it held. Theo had a few shirts, pants, and shorts that he commonly wore. Why did anyone need so many outfits?

"Aha," the maid said. "Here it is."

She exited the closet, carrying a colorful cloth, which she unfolded to show Theo. He covered his mouth and opened his eyes wide, thinking, *Surely, I don't have to wear* that! Bright red, orange, and blue tones screamed at him from the cloth.

He pleaded with the maid with his eyes. "It … it looks like something a circus clown would wear."

"How can you say such a thing? It's your father's." She glanced at the cloak. "Oh, *pft*. It's inside out." She turned the cloak around to reveal a royal blue fabric.

An image of the Znahar Tree had been embroidered onto it with silver thread. Light caught the material, making it shine like the Firebird and casting a rainbow of colors around the room.

"Now, that's something I wouldn't mind wearing," Theo said as he ran his fingers along the silky material.

"Not with what you have on." The maid *tsk*ed again and shook her head. She poked at Theo's stained T-shirt, snorted at his faded, holey pants, and let out an exasperated sigh at his dusty sneakers. She waved him toward the closet. "Go put on a white shirt, pants, and shoes that fit."

Theo sighed and looked at Ula. She just smirked and stifled laughter. He entered the closet and picked up the required items, trying them in front of himself to find ones that were the right size. Loaded down with the apparel, Theo slipped to the back of the closet, shed his dirty clothes, and slipped on the new ones. He didn't feel royal.

I guess this will have to do. He exited the closet and stood still while the maid walked around him, appraising his appearance.

"I reckon that's the best we can do." She sighed as she mimicked Theo's thoughts before she handed him the cloak. "Put this on, and we'll see if it improves matters."

Theo did as he was told, clasping the high-necked cloak at his throat. The maid's eyes sparkled, and a smile lit her face. "Much better. You now look like a king's son, the offspring of our beloved Zmey and Zunitza."

Ula nodded her agreement and gave Theo's forearm a squeeze. "You'll enter Kaleto a prince and leave as a king. Go look at yourself in the mirror." She pointed toward the back of the room.

A boy dressed in royal robes peered back at him. He was stronger, and a bit more muscular arms had replaced Theo's scrawny chicken ones, although he still had a long way to go to be muscle bound. He'd grown taller since his first visit to

Zmeykovo, and his baby face had morphed into something more serious. Despite the changes, in his heart he was the same boy. The Theo of Selo remained hidden under the marvelous clothes.

A gentle breeze tickled his cheeks. "*My handsome royal son.*" Zunitza's murmured words gave him courage. For the briefest of moments, her smiling face appeared in the mirror.

Pavel peeked into the room. "Hey, Theo, your chariot awaits." He broke into laughter when Theo turned around. "Oh, man. You look like the Little Prince."

Theo thanked the maid for helping him. On his way out, he punched Pavel lightly on the shoulder. "Try to be serious."

"How can I when you look like that?" Pavel smirked.

From behind them, Ula said, "Yes, fun's over. We have a battle to think about."

Pavel spun the weapon Sitara had given him. "I really love this dagger, and I want to help save Diva and get the apple and belt back, but man, I wish I had time to design a secret weapon. I don't have any magical powers like the rest of you."

"You have the magic of friendship," Theo said. "That's powerful by itself."

"Friendship doesn't keep people alive, though."

"You don't have to—"

"Stop right now. Don't even say it." Pavel scowled. "I'm not going to be left behind. I might be just a human, but I can think fast. I'll be as safe as the rest of you."

"I didn't mean—"

"Yes, you did. At least subconsciously. You keep trying to protect me."

Pavel was right. Theo did try to protect his friend. He couldn't bear any more losses. But it wasn't because Pavel was human. Theo wanted to protect Diva, too, and she had a lot of power. He didn't know what he would do if he lost either of them.

They walked in silence the rest of the way to the front gate. The carriage they'd ridden in before had been repaired, and the two Konedrakoni were decked out. Their feathery manes were braided with silver threads, and green crystals glittered along their length. Silver shields protected the beasts' scaled, muscle-bound chests, and war helmets covered their heads. The animals tossed their manes and spewed out short bursts of flames.

One of the coachmen held the door open for Theo. He entered the carriage alone. Loneliness overcame him as he made himself comfortable on the soft, plush seat. It had been crowded with Diva, Pavel, and all their gear the first time, but he much preferred that to being separated from his friends. It had to be this way. They couldn't risk having the others travel with him and making a stop at the secret entrance. Theo didn't know whether spies watched his every move, but it certainly felt like it.

At their last meeting, everyone had agreed that they'd travel to the location Drakus had told them about. The Samodivi would fly as birds, and the others on the winged deer: Pavel on Whirl, Sitara on Shar, and Jega on his own deer companion. Drakus had already said he'd meet them inside the fortress. Theo signaled to the coachman to leave. The dying rays of the sun painted the sky a rosy hue as Theo waved goodbye to his friends.

With no one around, Theo took advantage of the silence. He thought about Selo, about Nia and his human mother. He'd had little time to wonder what was going on in his village. Had his family given him up for dead? Theo's stomach ached to think of the pain he'd once again put his mother through. He missed her and Nia so much.

Closing his eyes, he tried to picture their faces, but Zima, dying and bloody on the ground, kept popping up. And along with that, Jega wailing at his brother's side. Theo would never again hear the banter of the two Kukeri brothers. And how would Mraz take it when he learned about Zima's death?

Theo sighed. He was needed here. It was necessary to put his personal needs and feelings about his family aside. He'd have time for that when Zlo and Lamia were defeated.

A soft *thud* made Theo look out the window. The Konedrakoni had landed and trotted along a cobblestone road. Up ahead, a craggy hillside, spotted with trees, loomed behind Kaleto Fortress. Theo and his friends had traversed the strangely shaped rocks on those cliffs the first time they had accessed the fortress. This current entrance was much easier, though likely as dangerous. Four guards, with arrows nocked and pointed toward the gate, stood within a watchtower. The structure was half hidden by fog and held a purplish-green glow.

More guards with swords crossed protected a gated stone arch. The creatures had a robotic look about them, but not in a calculated, organized way. They looked as if someone had put them together from a mishmash of parts discarded in a junkyard.

The body had a Hulk-like appearance, but was silver and brown instead of green. Spikes shot off in all directions. Even the hands ended in spiked fingers.

The creatures' heads had the typical elongated alien shape. The hair—if it was hair—had a feathered look, parted in the middle and sweeping in cornrows to each side. This hair covered the upward slanting eyes, which appeared to be permanently squinted. For a mouth, the beast had a gaping rectangular hole in its square jaw. It looked like a toy where a child matched shapes to holes.

Bony legs were like metal bars, and the joints connecting them to the feet had a triangular shape. They twisted and turned as the guards walked. Their feet looked like rake tines, the metal kind, only the tips of these were sharp and pointed.

Whatever they were, the creatures were creepy.

One of the coachmen from the silver carriage dismounted and showed the guards Theo's invitation. The guard looked at the parchment, peered inside the carriage, and cranked a wheel. The fortress gate creaked open, and the guard waved them through.

The carriage slowed and bounced along as it passed under the arch into a tunnel, which came out into the courtyard a few hundred feet ahead. Proceeding a short distance farther, the carriage stopped in front of black metal doors recessed between two massive stone towers. More guards stood in front, blocking the entrance. Above the doors, two Navi perched on a ledge. Their eyes locked on all who dared enter.

Theo had arrived at Zlo and Lamia's lair.

A coachman stepped down from his bench and opened the carriage doors so Theo could exit. The man handed Theo his invitation. He wrapped the princely cloak tight around his body as if it were a shield to protect him from the demons. Then he strode forward with what he hoped was a royal pace and handed one of the guards the parchment. The man looked it over. His mouth twitched as he handed it back, but he grasped the thick metal rungs on the door and pulled it open.

Scalding air hit Theo as he stepped inside the fortress. *Descending into Hades would probably be more appealing.*

"Wait here," the guard told him and disappeared farther into the fortress. He returned moments later with a woman dressed in purple. She wore a dragon mask.

"Follow me to the ceremony hall," she said, her voice even, but unemotional.

Theo hesitated but had no choice. He had already entered his enemy's domain.

They traveled down torch-lit corridors. Mirrors scattered along the way reflected the flickering light, making Theo feel as if he were passing through a portal to the underworld. His guide made so many turns, he felt lost. He counted the passageways they passed, checking for the painting Drakus had told him about. It hadn't appeared by the time Theo reached the number of corridors he recalled were on the map.

Sweat soaked his body, and his stomach gurgled as acid attempted to make its way up. He was going to have to go it alone if he couldn't find the place where his friends hid. A few more steps and another corridor loomed ahead. Theo used his dragon vision to peer at a painting. He let out a long breath. It was of the Ispolini. That had to be the right place. He hoped the picture hadn't been moved from where Drakus said it should have been.

"Excuse me, miss. I had a long journey. Is there somewhere I can freshen up?" His stomach grumbled again. "Some place with a bathroom?"

The masked woman stopped. "Of course. I'm sorry I didn't think to offer you that when you first came in. The closest restroom is down the corridor just ahead. Follow me."

They turned into the hallway past the painting, and the woman pointed to a door. "It's in there. I'll wait here for you."

Theo entered the room and bolted the door behind him. He scanned the room for the closet, finding it half hidden behind a mirror. According to Drakus, the door Theo had to unlock was inside the closet. He turned on a faucet to muffle any noise he might make. When he opened the closet door, brooms and brushes toppled out and littered the floor.

"Is everything all right?" the woman outside asked.

"Yes, everything's fine," Theo called out.

At the back of the closet, he discovered a second door hidden by towels, outfits, and other materials. He slowly unbolted it. It scraped along, rusted from what must have been ages of disuse.

"Is anyone down there?" Theo whispered into the massive pipe. His words bounced around the sides, echoing as they traveled down.

Pavel's voice sounded miles away when he replied, "We're here. Everything's going according to plan. We'll see you soon."

"There are clean, dry clothes in the closet," Theo said. "They seem to be all sizes, so everyone should find something that fits. I have to go now before my guide gets suspicious."

Theo pulled a chain above the toilet, and water poured down. Not super modern, but it worked. He hoped Drakus was right, and the hidden pipe wasn't for sewerage. Pavel would have words to say to Theo if the water he flushed just poured down on them.

The woman knocked on the door. "Are you okay in there?"

"Yes, coming." Theo washed his hands and dried them on a towel.

He exited the bathroom and followed the purple-clad woman. The ballroom lay just ahead. The woman bowed to guards standing in front of the room, and they opened the massive wooden doors. Blood-red light spilled across the room, making it look like a scene from a horror movie.

"Welcome, *dear nephew*. So glad you could make it." A wicked grin grew on Theo's aunt's face.

Only it wasn't Lamia who had spoken.

It was Magda.

"We have so much entertainment for you tonight."

Chapter 19
Secrets, Secrets

THEO SAW RED, and it wasn't because that color dominated the ballroom. Boiling hot anger pulsed through his blood. Anger at himself for being deceived. Anger at those who had deceived him. Not only anger, but questions. He couldn't force his legs to move forward. Jumbled thoughts about his aunt paralyzed him as they vied for the most attention in his mind.

If Magda is here, who's taking care of Zmey? Ula and Sava had traveled with his other friends and were waiting in the tunnel pipe. None of the others in the castle had even the slightest ability to tend to their king.

Wasn't Magda terrified of Lamia? She had most definitely acted that way on the terrace when Lamia arrived. Had it all been a show, a red herring, to throw suspicion onto someone else as far as Diva's departure was concerned?

And the thought that continued to wrack his brain the most: *What is Magda's motive for helping Lamia?*

He feared he was about to discover the answers. But more than that, his gut told him that what he learned would devastate him.

The red faded from Theo's mind as dread overtook him. Still, the room was awash with a reddish glow. It came from the stained-glass window above the throne. Gone was the ruby-red dragon's eye that had been instrumental in Lamia's resurrection and the release of demons into Zmeykovo. Theo had shattered that window, preventing the demons from escaping into the human world. A new image replaced the former one. Still red, it displayed a bloody heart pierced by an arrow.

What does it mean? Lost love? A broken heart? Did Lamia even have a heart at all? Theo couldn't help but think that maybe it was a message to him. His own heart would be pierced.

The rest of the room slowly came back into focus. The empty throne, where the Evil One, Lord Zlo, had once sat. *Where is he? And Lamia, too?* The two beasts who caused so much trouble hadn't made their presence known—yet.

Others besides Magda crowded the room, though. And they weren't demons. Courtiers were lined up on either side of the throne. Had they also become traitors to their king, the way the Knights of Darkness had? Or had these guests been coerced or enchanted? One thing was sure: they would present a problem if Theo and his friends had to battle Zlo and Lamia. Theo didn't want harm to come to innocent, unarmed people.

A sharp point poked into the back of Theo's neck. He'd let his guard down. Too surprised by Magda's presence and Lamia's absence. A warrior held a sword, ready to end Theo's life.

"It seems we have an intruder," the voice said.

Theo didn't have to turn to know who it belonged to. Radan. Zlo's commander of his army of demons.

Now would be a good time for Theo's friends to arrive.

The tip of the sword moved along Theo's neck as the warrior stepped within Theo's line of sight. Radan was covered with black metal armor and a helmet the way he had been the first time Theo had set eyes on the beast. The antlers that jutted out of the side of his head and his long anteater-like snout still made Theo cringe. Radan's icy-blue eyes bore into Theo.

The creature leaned closer, snarling. "There's nothing I'd like better than to stuff my sword down you now and make you into a shish kabob. Unfortunately, I'd lose my head if I did so without Zlo's command."

"Radan, enough," Magda shouted. "Theo is on the honored guest list. He's not an enemy. Lamia has invited our dear nephew to celebrate with her."

Theo cringed at Magda's use once again of Lamia's backhanded term of endearment. He had thought Magda had some sense of family concern. If not for him, at least for his father. She had, after all, taken care of Zmey since his rescue. But now, he realized it had all been fake. Why had she bothered to help Zmey at all? She could easily have let him die, let Lamia have all of Zmey's power right away. Theo wanted to ask questions, get answers. Right now, though, he had to play along with the game and pretend he threw his support to Lamia.

Radan growled as he withdrew his sword. "Your aunt, both of them, may have taken pity on you, but I haven't. I won't forget the trouble you've caused. One step out of line and ..." He let the threat hang in the air.

The creature kept a tight grip on his sword, rather than sheathing it, as he stomped toward the other side of the ballroom.

Theo rubbed his neck, feeling sticky moisture. He drew back his hand and wished he still wore his dirty shirt, so he could wipe the spot of blood on it. Plastering on a fake smile to match Magda's, he replied, "Yes, I came for her special ceremony."

He was here for the ceremony all right, but not to celebrate. Theo was determined to stop Lamia from consuming the apple. Even though it made him want to vomit, he could pretend he was Lamia's ally and that he'd come with good intentions.

"Bravo. It's nice to see you come to your senses," Magda said.

"But why are *you* here?" Theo asked. "I thought you were terrified of Lamia."

"Don't you just love the charades we put on?" Magda laughed. "You thought I was truly afraid of her? How delicious. I have another surprise for you. A special guest."

She whispered to a Youda lurking in the shadows and pointed to a corner. The woman nodded and retreated to a room, the same place where Zlo had kept Kosara captive.

Theo's breath quickened. Had these monsters captured the priestess again? But how? The dome around the Znahar Tree was the safest place in Zmeykovo.

A moment later, the Youda returned, escorting the "guest."

Theo froze. It wasn't Kosara. It was Diva. Following her were the Knights of Darkness. They formed a protective semicircle behind her.

Diva's pale face was highlighted by the white dress she wore that was embroidered with glowing silver designs. They appeared to be runes, rather than the usual embellishments of the Firebird or Znahar Tree. Her wild, curly hair had been braided and decorated with a floral wreath. She looked even more lovely than normal, garbed as a princess.

But her face was expressionless, her eyes lifeless. She looked straight at Theo but gave no indication she saw or recognized him. The runes on her garment were likely the culprit, keeping his friend enchanted. That seemed to be a specialty of Zlo's, to trap his enemies inside their own minds, living the lies the evil demon lord chose to make them believe.

The Youda brought Diva to stand by Magda's side. The contrast between the purity of Diva's appearance to Magda's, dressed as she was in a crimson dress, trimmed with gold, made Theo's dragon spirit stir. The beast inside him roared.

"What have you done to her?" He stormed forward, but the tip of a sword pressed into his stomach. Radan, the creepy second-in-command, had made his way back across the ballroom.

"She's my devoted servant." Magda smirked. "Like you, she came to her senses and acknowledged me as queen."

Magda nodded again to the Youda, and the woman placed a crown upon Magda's head. It was the same one Theo had seen in his mother's portrait.

"Queen?" Theo snorted.

"Yes, queen of the Samodivi."

"Zunitza was a queen. She—"

"My sister should never have been queen!" Magda screeched.

"Zunitza's people loved her." Theo bared his teeth at Magda. "You are nothing … an impostor."

"No, she is the one who was the imposter." Magda's eyes filled with fiery flames. "As the elder twin, I should have been queen. I should have been the one to marry your stupid father. I loved him so much, but he was under my sister's spell. If he had married me, everything would have been wonderful."

Theo's heart ached with the insanity of Magda's jealousy. "You can wear a crown and play make-believe, just like you did with my mother's wedding dress, but no one in their right mind will do your bidding."

"Oh, but they will. Lamia will make sure they do."

It all made sense now to Theo. Magda's motivation. Lamia had promised Magda the right to rule the Samodivi if she helped. And somehow Magda had forced Diva to steal the Golden Apple. Couldn't Magda have done it herself when everyone was asleep? Why involve Diva? That didn't make any sense. Unless it was just some cruel joke to make Theo doubt his friend.

Magda was still talking, but Theo didn't care to listen to anything else she had to say. He was eager to have Lamia arrive. He'd show her what he thought of her plans. He itched to take his sword out of its sheath and put an end to his aunt—both of them— right now. But he knew he couldn't do that quite yet.

"Are you listening?" Magda screeched at him.

"No. I'm not interested in what you have to say." Theo chastised himself for having ever felt sorry for the life Magda had led. It was all a lie. Told just to toy with him. The same way Lamia did.

Magda laughed. "Oh, I'm sure you'll want to hear this. When Zunitza gave birth to you in the human world, it was the saddest moment in my life. I wanted to hold the child she held to her breast, a child who should have been born to me. A child who would have loved me." Magda cradled her arms and rocked, as if she was lulling an infant to sleep.

Theo could almost feel compassion for Magda. Almost. But he wouldn't allow himself to because of what she had done to Diva … and for whatever truth she was about to reveal. Dread was building in his heart, and he began to sweat.

Magda's eyes went hard, and she dropped her arms. "I wanted so much to be my sister, but I was nothing more than a slave to her."

"I doubt that." Theo snorted.

"I was. Zunitza took from me. She took the man I loved. She took the kingdom. She took my self-esteem. But I paid her back." Fire danced in Magda's eyes. "I took something precious from her, and she never knew it."

"What did you do, you evil witch?" Theo shook. Had she harmed Zunitza? Was she the actual one who killed his mother? He'd believed Zunitza had died fighting after she returned to Zmeykovo.

"Your mother was in so much pain after giving birth to you, and I relished her moans." A maniacal laugh left Magda's lips. "Two other Samodivi had accompanied your mother and me to the human world, so we could place her child in a safe home when it was born. I sent both of the women far off to find herbs that I told them would ease your mother's pain."

Theo breathed deeply to slow his racing heart. It thumped loudly in his ears. He didn't want to know, yet he did. What had Magda done?

His aunt said, "I used herbs I had on me to make your mother unconscious. You see, she still had another child in her belly. A girl was soon born."

"I … I have a sister?"

As if she didn't hear Theo, Magda continued her tale, "This was my moment of revenge. I took the child and returned to Zmeykovo. I didn't care what the other Samodivi thought about me abandoning Zunitza. As far as I was concerned, she and her boy—you—could die before they returned. I couldn't let them know there was another child."

"How could you? What did you do with my sister?" Theo narrowed his eyes. He took a step toward Magda, but Radan pressed his sword deeper into Theo's flesh.

"Ah ha ha." Magda laughed. "This is the fun part. I brought her to the demon forest. I was certain predators would devour such tender flesh. Red eyes glowed all around, and the infant screamed. I was elated. It hadn't taken long."

"You … you … you …" Theo wanted to vomit. Magda had maliciously murdered his sister, a sister he never knew. That was worse than whatever had torn Zmey and Lamia apart. To do that to an innocent baby …

"I knew I recognized you from somewhere." Drakus' voice brought Theo out of his dark place.

When had the Oupir arrived? Theo turned his head toward the doorway. All of his friends were here: Jega, Sitara, Pavel, Ula, and Sava. They were dressed in clothes similar to those of Lamia's courtiers and blended in with the other guests. The Knights of Darkness held Theo's friends at bay, but Theo didn't think they were any more capable of moving than he was at the moment. Their eyes were filled with the same horror Theo felt.

Drakus continued, "I was there on that cold, eerie night when you left the infant, and I'm the one who made her scream."

"Noooo!" Theo clenched his stomach.

Drakus broke away from the Knights of Darkness and came to stand by Theo. "After that coward ran away, I found the basket she left behind. I hadn't eaten in ages, but when I saw that tiny being, my hunger left me. Her eyes pierced my soul and cold heart and reminded me of my beloved Lora—before she was changed."

"So, you didn't …" Theo couldn't say the words.

"No." Drakus shook his head. "I gathered up the basket and brought her to the safest place I could think of. I left her under the Znahar Tree in Kosara's care. I never knew what happened to her."

Ula and Sava looked at each other, and then Sava said, "We do. Kosara brought the girl to the temple, and then Bendis gave her to us to raise. That baby was Diva."

Chapter 20
From Gold to Ash

THEO'S HEAD SPUN. Diva was his sister. His twin. All this time, he'd felt a connection to her, yet he'd never known they had a blood relationship. It made sense why they could communicate with one another through their minds. And now she was like a zombie, mindless, standing by Magda.

"What did you do to my sister?" Theo gripped the hilt of his sword, wanting so much to pull it from its sheath.

"It didn't take much to put her under a dark spell that none of you can break." Magda wrapped her arm around Diva's shoulder. "She nicely obliged me by taking a sip of the water I gave her. That allowed me to command her whenever I chose. Now she belongs to me."

"Let her go, you old witch!" Pavel yelled from the back of the room.

Theo spun around. The Knights of Darkness had formed a tight circle around his friends. Pavel pulled out his dagger and rushed one of his captors. The man knocked the weapon away with a flick of his wrist. Pavel then kicked the man and pounded his chest, but the warrior stood his ground, unlikely to cause more harm until he was commanded to do so.

Radan remained in front of Theo, and archers had gathered around the perimeter of the room, pointing their arrows at him and Drakus. They were surrounded, but Theo would find a way to get past them. Magda would pay. Once Lamia and Zlo arrived, they all would pay.

As if on cue, a guard at the door announced, "Lamia has arrived."

Surrounded by her retinue, Lamia entered the ballroom, carried on a canopy-covered litter. As she passed Theo, she motioned for the servants to stop.

"*Dear nephew*, I see you took great care to look like a prince to honor me on this special day." She stroked his cheek with her claws, and he shuddered. She leaned closer and under her breath said, "But I'm so disappointed in you for bringing your friends. That tells me you plan to disrupt my ceremony. I thought you'd be smart enough to assist me. Now, whatever happens is your own fault."

Lamia clicked her claws, and the litter bearers took a step forward.

"I told you I'd never work with you." Theo glared at her and grabbed hold of his aunt's arm to stop the litter from advancing. "Did you know Diva is my sister?"

She laughed. "Of course. I know all the secrets. The ones that happened here in Zmeykovo, and those that happened in the human world, in your precious Selo."

"Why did you keep it a secret?"

"I did try to warn you about her, that she'd betray you."

"She didn't betray me!" Theo shouted. "Magda cursed Diva."

"Oh, tut, tut. Such a temper." She shook off Theo's hand. "Enough talk. It's time for the ceremony. Once I take a bite from the Golden Apple, I'll have the universe in my hands. I'm grateful to you for your courage to harvest the apple from the sacred tree, and then so kindly deliver it into my hands."

"I didn't! Why would I do anything to help you become more powerful?" He wanted to kill her now, but where was Zlo? Theo needed to stop them all. And he needed his father's belt.

Lamia clicked her claws again, and the servants proceeded to the throne and placed the litter on the floor. She slithered off, ascended the steps to the throne, and curled her snake tail around herself after she sat. The servants and gathered guests arranged themselves in two half circles around Lamia.

A gong sounded from somewhere, and a servant dressed in black carried in the round golden box into which Kosara had placed the Golden Apple. With slow, steady steps in time to the beat of the gong, the man approached the throne. He kneeled before Lamia and held out the box.

Lamia slid off of the throne, grasped the box, and held it over her head. She gazed up toward the dome of the ballroom. "My Master, my Lord, we are ready for the ceremony."

Theo followed Lamia's gaze. A mass of black smoke with a fiery red flashing core swirled down from the dome. Many of the attendees gasped and cowered, backing away from the throne. To Theo, the apparition looked like a portal to Hades. But he knew what it really was. He'd seen it before. Lord Zlo, Lamia's master.

Lamia continued her speech, if that's what she considered it was. Theo thought she was just putting on a show to those she'd likely coerced into attending. She performed like the man behind the curtain in the land of Oz.

Her voice rose higher as Lord Zlo descended. "When I take the power of the apple, we will rule the world, my Lord. We can enter the human world at will and enslave the entire population. My brother won't be able to stop us. Nor will the moon goddess or the sun god. We will become like the deities. We will be all-powerful. We …"

On and on she went, and Theo tuned her out. His gaze remained on the black orb. It spun even more furiously, and the fiery core took on the shape of a face with a mouth filled with sharp teeth. Horns appeared next, jutting up on the monster's head. The creature let out a demonic laugh. People screamed and covered their ears.

Theo tried to think of a way to destroy Zlo. Having fought against the beast before, Theo recalled how Zlo had disappeared into the same black mist that circled above. Theo's sword had held no power over that dark energy. Zlo had to have some weakness, though, and Theo would discover it.

"It's time." Lamia lowered the golden box and opened it.

The apple inside glowed, illuminating her face, which contorted as her eyes sparked with malice. Theo was too far away to feel the apple's pull the way he had when he'd harvested it. And he was glad. He didn't want it making him crazed for power.

Lamia held the apple aloft. "Behold the Golden Apple. It holds the power of the world, which will soon be mine." She looked toward Magda and said, "Now!"

Magda took a knife that the Youda standing next to her offered. With the weapon, Magda sliced Diva across the palm.

"Stop!" Theo shouted, and Pavel screamed. Hisses came from Sava and Ula.

Strong arms gripped Theo from behind, preventing him from dashing to help Diva. By the nauseating stench, Theo knew it was Bor Stobor. Guards surrounded Drakus, as well, but stayed out of the Oupir's reach. He glared at the men, and their legs trembled, but neither Drakus nor the soldiers moved from their place.

"Silence!" Lamia shouted.

Magda brought the bloody knife to Lamia and bowed as she backed away, to return to her place next to Diva.

"With the blood of the female heir to the throne," Lamia chanted, "I now transfer the royal bloodline to myself when I consume this golden fruit." She sliced the apple with the knife. Without any more delay, Lamia brought the Golden Apple to her mouth. Her snake tongue darted out With a final triumphant look at Theo, she slowly licked the apple.

"No!" came from all corners of the room. Theo struggled to free himself from Bor Stobor's iron grasp, but the Karakonjul held fast.

"Drakus, do something!" Theo shouted at the Oupir, who still stood unencumbered next to Theo. "Lamia's going to eat the apple, and we'll all be doomed!"

Drakus opened his mouth to say something, but a whistling drowned out his words. A blinding flash followed. People screamed and covered their eyes. His jaw slack, Theo stared as the apple burst into thousands of pieces. White ash exploded over the guests and floated down, coating everyone.

The black cloud that was Lord Zlo twisted furiously and flashed like lightning. A gale storm filled the room, tossing people to the walls and floor. The floating ash whirled like a blizzard. Screams of pain and fear sounded from every corner.

Lord Zlo began to emerge from the swirling cloud and shouted at Lamia, "You've failed me again."

"Don't punish me." Lamia dropped her face to the floor. "This has to be my brother's fault. I'll find the real apple. It's mine. It's ours."

"Prove that you can handle your pathetic brother."

"Don't talk about my father like that." Theo continued to struggle against Bor Stobor.

Lord Zlo completely formed out of the swirling blackness and walked toward Lamia. Then everything turned crazy.

Bor Stobor grunted and loosened his hold on Theo.

Drakus charged toward Lord Zlo.

Theo drew his sword.

Pavel head-butted a soldier who turned to look toward the commotion.

Sava and Ula let fly arrows.

Jega let out an animalistic war cry.

Sitara slammed together the heads of two Knights of Darkness.

Magda grabbed hold of Diva and scrambled to a wall.

In the space of a few seconds, a colony of fire-winged bats whirled around Zlo. Faster and faster, they surrounded the demon lord, tightening the circle.

Lamia lifted her head from the floor, but remained where she was. She signaled for the Knights of Darkness to hold off on attacks. She kept her eyes peeled on the flying bats. Theo couldn't tell if it was hope or despair that glinted in her eyes.

Zlo's voice sounded loud in Theo's mind above the chaos in the room. But the demon's words were not meant for Theo. They were spoken to Drakus. *"Spare my life, Oupir, and I will make an offering to you, anything you wish."*

"I cannot."

"But you know you must. Your curse requires you to accept." In Theo's mind, Zlo's words held a soothing, hypnotic edge, but were laced with fear. *"What is your deepest desire?"*

"I want …" Even in thoughts, Drakus' voice choked. *"I want both Lora and myself to be restored to what we were before our curses."*

Zlo continued in his quiet voice. *"I can do only one. Choose wisely."*

"Lora." Drakus sobbed. *"Free Lora from her curse."*

"It is done. Now release me."

The swirling bats slowed their pace, and Theo caught glimpses of Zlo within the circle. As the bats lessened their assault, Zlo began to re-form into a black mist.

"No!" Theo shouted. "You won't escape this time."

The words Theo had kept hearing earlier in the week came back to him: *He who has light within himself will tear apart the darkness.*

Why hadn't he remembered that earlier? Bendis had given Theo that light, both in himself and in his sword. He pointed his weapon into the gaps the bats made. Holding his fingers over the symbol of the sun that had been newly etched into the sword's hilt, Theo called on Tangra's power. The sword glowed white, and a light beam shot out from the tip into the growing darkness. An unearthly scream came from Zlo a moment before the black mist dissipated.

The room became deathly quiet. No one moved. Finally, Lamia rose from the floor and slithered toward Magda.

With a roar, Lamia struck Magda in the face. "You traitor! You dare bring me a fake apple!"

"I didn't. I'm innocent," Magda screamed.

Lamia grabbed Magda by the neck and squeezed. "What kind of deal did you make with my brother? Did he promise to wed you? You'll make a poor substitute for his true bride. He'll never love you."

Writhing within Lamia's grasp, Magda gasped out, "That was the apple Diva stole. She must have replaced it."

Theo couldn't believe what he heard. Somehow Diva must have known about Magda's treachery and brought the fake apple with her to the harvesting ceremony. Theo had been so exhausted when he went to sleep that it would have been easy for her to switch the apples. But then, where had she hidden the real one?

"Where is it? Where is the true Golden Apple?" Lamia's words reflected Theo's thoughts, but his aunt was asking Magda, not Diva.

"I don't know. I told you already."

"You lie!" Lamia screeched, her face contorting. Scales covered her face and hands. "You'll never be queen of the Samodivi. I'll kill you first." She smacked the crown from Magda's head.

As soon as Lamia removed her hand from Magda's throat, Magda turned into a black snake and slithered away into a crack in the wall.

Theo couldn't help but laugh at the soap-opera drama. "Everyone's abandoned you. Your master left you to take care of your mess. Your patsy betrayed you. Neither one cared anything about you, only the power you could give them. Now you're all alone."

"I'm not alone." Lamia looked around the room. The Knights of Darkness appeared dazed and had broken their circle around Theo's friends. Radan and Bor Stobor had already fled. All the guests had somehow managed to quietly slip away from the room.

"Seize them. Kill them all!" Lamia shouted, but no one moved to obey her.

"See, no friends," Theo taunted.

"I can still cause you pain. Perhaps not enough blood was shed on the apple tonight. I'll rectify that." Lamia grew, her body tearing apart as she shifted into a three-headed dragon. "*It's time to solve one family problem once and for all and take something precious from you and your father*," she thought to Theo.

"No!" Theo rushed forward to stop Lamia.

His aunt swung her sword-sharp tail and stabbed Diva in the chest with one blow. Diva swayed and fell to the floor, red seeping over her dress. The floral wreath fell next to her, bathed in blood.

Chapter 21
Sorrow Upon Sorrow

THEO CRADLED DIVA'S lifeless body in his arms, rocking her in time to his moans. He had removed his fancy cloak and laid it over her. Pavel sat next to them. His fingers lightly stroked Diva's red-stained hair. He gulped in air through his sobs. Fog coated his glasses, and sweat beaded on his face.

Diva's sisters stood around them, anger and grief etched into their faces. The Samodivi kept their eyes on Diva, but Theo could tell they were alert to their enemies in the room. Sitara, Jega, and Drakus kept their focus on Lamia and the Knights of Darkness. The warriors stumbled around as if unsure of where they were.

Kosara had told Theo that darkness surrounded him and he would have to suffer more sorrows. He'd never imagined it would be watching a sister die. He'd lost her before either one of them had ever known they were twins. Kosara had also said his sorrows would make him stronger. The Thracian deities had found him "worthy," in the priestess' words.

Theo couldn't help thinking, *If holding a deceased loved one in your arms is what being worthy means, I'd rather be a scoundrel. I'll make Lamia pay, Diva. I won't let her get away with all the pain she's caused everyone.* His tears dripped onto Diva's face.

As gently as he could, Theo laid Diva back onto the floor. He stood and wiped her blood onto his shirt. The irony of it. He'd been afraid to dirty his clothing earlier with a few drops of blood. Now, he was covered with that of his sister.

"How touching." All three of Lamia's beastly heads smirked, looking even more menacing coming from a dragon's face.

"You!" Theo stomped toward his aunt. He wanted to slice her to bits, but his hands shook too much from grief. "Why? Why did you kill her? She's your flesh and blood."

"Oh, tut, tut. She's always been a thorn in my side. I just gave her a thorn back." Lamia laughed as she swung her sharp-pointed tail toward Theo. *"I've allowed you your moment so I could enjoy your pain. How does it feel to suffer? Now you know what it's like to lose someone you love with all your heart."*

"You're a monster!" Theo shouted. "I don't believe you ever knew how to love anyone."

"Enough talk! It's time for you to join your sister. I'll put an end to Zmey and Zunitza's love story, as well as their dynasty." Lamia opened her giant maws and spewed fire toward Theo.

He rolled out of the way. Sitara, Drakus, and Jega were there in a flash, stabbing at Lamia, to keep her at bay. A clatter sounded at the ballroom door. The Knights of Darkness were picking up their weapons. Their eyes had darkened, and their countenances grown stern. Whatever had muddled their brains earlier was gone.

The warriors sounded a battle cry, and dashed forward. Bor Stobor and Radan had returned as well.

Theo shouted, "Go fight them, but can one of you keep Lamia occupied for a moment?"

"I will." Drakus didn't wait for objections. He spun into a whirlwind. A flutter of black wings emerged, and hundreds of bats swarmed Lamia.

Jega and Sitara joined the Samodivi, who had already begun shooting arrows at their enemies.

After the Oupir's earlier betrayal in letting Zlo go, Theo hoped Drakus wouldn't do the same with Lamia. Not having time to worry about it, Theo ran back to where Pavel had dragged Diva to a corner, away from the fighting, and protectively stood in front of her, wielding a sword he must have picked up when the Knights of Darkness were confused.

"Will you try to get Diva out of here?" Unwilling to think of her as dead, Theo couldn't bear to say *her body*. "Will you get Ula or Sava to take her somewhere safe?"

Ula raced over and picked up Diva. "I'll bring her to Samodivi Lake. Sava will stay here to fight."

"I'm not leaving Diva," Pavel said.

"Good." Theo laid his hand on his friend's shoulder. "Thank you for protecting my … sister. I knew I could count on you."

"Watch out, Theo." Pavel pushed Theo aside as a sword sliced through the air where his head had been.

Radan had broken through the fighting. He growled and prepared to stab Theo. An arrow pierced the man's shoulder, and he let out a roar.

"Go!" Theo shouted to Pavel and Ula. "I'll handle him now."

As they crept along the wall, making their way to the exit, Theo bellowed to his dragon spirit, *"Let's show them who's boss."*

His shoulders expanded, and his legs became stout and filled with strength. Radan drew his sword and turned his attack toward Pavel and Ula, but Theo had completed his shift to a dragon. He thrust his powerful tail at Radan, hurling the beast against a group of Knights of Darkness, toppling them all to the floor like dominoes.

Pavel and Ula escaped through the open doors. Once there, Pavel stopped and turned around.

In his mind, Theo said, *"Be safe,"* wishing his friend could hear him.

"We will. Thank you. I'll take care of Diva." Pavel opened his eyes wide, and Theo did, too.

For the first time, Pavel had been able to hear what Theo said when he was a dragon. It had to be because of the mental connection they had made when Theo entered Pavel's mind to rescue him from Sirin's song. Theo couldn't think about that now. He flapped his wings in a goodbye gesture as Pavel hurried after Ula.

Theo roared, and the room momentarily stilled. Drakus took his cue and flew off to help battle their other enemies.

As Theo stomped toward Lamia, he blocked out all other sights and sounds, so he could concentrate solely on her. Radan, Bor Stobor, and the Knights of Darkness could inflict only minor injuries on Theo now that he'd gained control of his powers. Only Lamia posed a threat.

"It's time, dear nephew, *to solve our problems once and forever."* Lamia launched toward Theo and exhaled flames from all three heads.

Theo pulled away, but the fire grazed his wing. He locked eyes with her in a fierce gaze. "*I couldn't agree more, dear aunt.*"

He'd barely spoken the words when Lamia lashed out with her massive spiked tail. A sharp pain pierced Theo's shoulder. He roared, shaking the room and causing Knights of Darkness to tumble to the floor. Theo leapt into the air. His scales glittered from the light of the torches in scones around the room. Coming up behind Lamia, he retaliated, scorching her golden scales with a blast of fire.

Lamia roared in fury. She spun around and launched herself into the air and charged Theo with her claws extended. Theo met her head-on. They clashed with a thunderous impact, shaking the room once more. Time and again, they slammed into each other, tearing at one another with teeth and claws.

Despite Theo's ferocity, Lamia had experienced more battles. She crashed into Theo again, sending him tumbling to the floor. Her massive jaws grabbed hold of his throat, biting him savagely. His strength began to falter beneath her weight and attack.

"*I need more power,*" Theo begged his dragon spirit. "*We can't let her win.*"

A surge of energy pulsed through his body. Theo roared with all his might. A shockwave rippled around the room, hurling Lamia into the wall. Marble shattered and an avalanche of stone exploded around the room. Shrieks came from the Knights of Darkness.

Theo shot up off of the floor and soared back into the air. He plunged toward Lamia, who lay stunned. Once more, the two fought, jaws snapping and claws slashing. After what seemed like an eternity of fierce combat, they both collapsed onto the floor. Puffs of smoke shot out of their maws with their heavy breathing.

Theo had to get her to switch back to her woman-snake form, so he could take the ouroboros belt from her. When she was a dragon, both belts were transformed into tattoos on her chest.

Think, Theo, he told himself. *How do I get her to switch back?*

Once before, she had shifted to a woman-snake when he'd used the sword's magic to freeze her flames. But he'd done that in human form. Now, he was a dragon.

She'd also changed from human to dragon when she'd been insulted. Her pride seemed to be her weak spot.

Will that work in reverse? Will her anger make her reckless?

It was worth a try.

Theo challenged Lamia. *"We're equally matched as dragons. If you're so strong, why don't you fight as a woman instead? Are you afraid I'd win, especially since your master isn't here to assist you?"*

She snorted and tossed her heads. *"I can win any battle against you, you feeble-minded boy. You're just like your father."*

Lamia shifted back to her woman appearance, and Theo returned to being a boy.

The sounds and smells of battle resumed: screaming, swords clashing, blood, burning flesh. The room shook with the clomping and pounding of footsteps against the marble floor. If Theo wanted to survive in this form, he had to be aware of everything that happened around him.

During her transformation, Lamia had acquired weapons, a spear and a nasty looking axe. *Neat trick*, he thought, *but they can't have the same power as my sword.*

Lamia held her weapons ready to attack, and Theo took a defensive stance, clutching his sword. She had told him once before that the sword couldn't harm her, but now it had more powers that Lamia didn't know about. Could they defeat her?

Theo focused on the ouroboros belt. A metal chain and lock had been looped through it, securing it to her waist. He pointed his sword toward the belt, but Lamia dissolved into black smoke. The slithering of her tail across the marble alerted him to the fact she was behind him. Before he could turn around, she slammed the end of her tail across his thighs, causing him to buckle. He fell, tucked, and rolled, barely missing having her crush his feet with her tail.

She dissolved into black smoke again. Theo couldn't see her, but he sensed her presence. A swish of air. He ducked, and the axe swept past him. He spun around to face her. Lamia's fingernails had turned into metal spikes, which she pointed toward his heart. She disappeared once more.

"Dragon spirit, help me see her."

A shadowy figure slithered toward him. Theo thrust his sword toward it. Light exploded, and Lamia screeched. The dark mist disappeared.

"Let's do it now," Theo commanded his dragon spirit.

He held his sword steady. It was time to use the abilities Bendis had bestowed upon the weapon. The power of the moon to draw forward and push away. Theo commanded his sword to do both. Blue light shot out and pushed Lamia into the wall. At the same time, the light wrapped around her body, spinning her. The lock burst open, the chain unraveled, and the ouroboros belt loosened.

Theo pulled it toward himself.

"No!" Lamia screeched and froze the belt mid-air.

It clattered to the floor.

Lamia hissed and ran to get the belt. At the same time, Drakus swung his black cloak around himself. A strong wind like a funnel blew into the ballroom, pushing Lamia back once more. Drakus' body turned into hundreds of bats that surrounded her, sticking to her body and tail.

"Let me go! Radan, help!" Lamia screamed. "Get the belt!"

Radan dashed forward, but Jega blocked his path with a fiery sword.

Theo dove and grabbed the belt. An arrow shot past him and pierced Lamia's shoulder. She screamed and wrenched out the arrow as she struck the bats that stuck to her like leeches.

In triumph, Theo held the belt for Lamia to see. "Now you can no longer hurt my father." He separated the two halves and dropped Lamia's onto the floor, but kept a tight grasp on his father's belt.

Drakus slowly returned to his former self.

"I have what I came for," he shouted to the Oupir. "Tell everyone to leave the way they came. I'll make sure Radan and the others don't follow."

Drakus nodded. As he rushed toward Theo's friends, Theo once more shifted into a dragon. He flew and blocked the entrance, breathing fire at their enemies to keep them back. The Knights of Darkness' swords pinched as they struck Theo, but none stuck in his scales. When his friends had enough time to return to their escape route, Theo looked for a way out.

It was déjà vu. It had to be the stained-glass window again.

With no other choice, he jumped and rushed to the window with all his strength. The bloody heart split into a thousand pieces, in the same way his heart had split when he saw Diva's lifeless body.

Chapter 22
Race Against Time

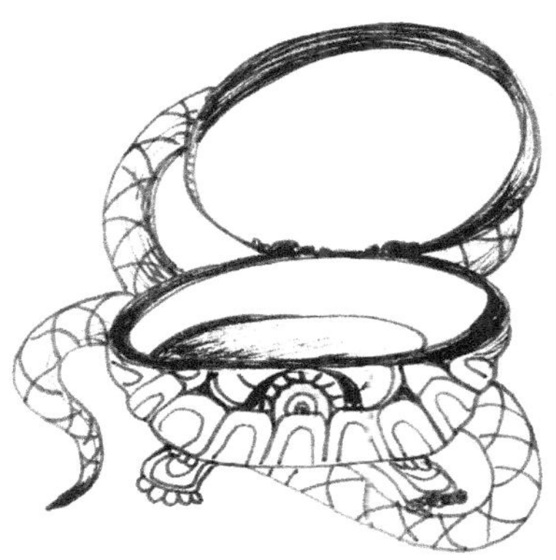

THE LOSS OF DIVA left Theo feeling powerless and alone. He blamed himself for what happened in Kaleto. There should have been something he could have done to prevent her death.

Why did I wait to attack Lamia? We could have fought Zlo later on. I didn't have to make sure both monsters were there.

He continued to blame himself the entire flight to the castle. For not paying attention, which had allowed Radan to approach. For not remembering about the sword's new powers until it was too late. For not … doing all the little details he didn't even know about.

And now his dear friend, his sister, had been killed.

Theo would mourn Diva properly later. Right now, he had a chance to save his father. He couldn't lose two family members in the same day. But he had to hurry. What was left of the belt's magic was seeping away into the night air, leaving a thin trail of sparkles. He rushed onward, clutching the precious ouroboros to his heart.

As he neared the castle, he detected a faint trace of his mother's voice. *"Hurry, my beloved son. Although I love your father, you must keep Zmey with you for a while longer."*

Theo circled the castle first, to ensure no enemy approached. All appeared safe, so he landed at the front gate and reverted to human form. Someone asked Theo a question as he raced into the castle. Without paying attention to what the person said, he rushed up the stairs and down corridors until he reached Zmey's door. Out of breath, he threw the door open and ran toward the bed.

He stopped short. A woman wearing red hunched over Zmey.

Has Magda returned? Is she trying to kill Zmey?

Theo hurled her away from his father. "What are you doing here, witch?"

The woman slammed against the wall. It was a witch, all right, but not the one he'd imagined.

Baba Yaga groaned as she pushed herself up from the floor. "I know you don't like me, but was that necessary?"

Theo turned his back on her, sensing her still huddled against the wall. "I don't have time for this right now. I have to save my father."

Baba Yaga grumbled, "That's what I was doing, keeping your father alive, since your aunt Magda disappeared." She adjusted the kerchief that had slipped down her shoulders. The material was decorated with red flowers, which Theo had thought was the dress Magda had worn to the ceremony.

Theo lifted his father to wrap the belt around his waist. Zmey had become gaunt once again, almost as emaciated as when Theo had discovered his father in prison. Had it all been because Lamia was sucking Zmey's lifeforce away with the belt? Or had Magda been accelerating the process? His aunt had shooed Theo away so many times, claiming Zmey was resting and shouldn't be disturbed.

For someone who said she loved Zmey, she didn't show it. Theo thought she would have had more compassion for a person she cared about. Obviously, what she considered "love" was merely an obsession. Theo doubted Magda had loved Zmey first as she claimed. It seemed more likely that she wanted Zmey because of her jealousy toward Zunitza. Whatever Theo's mother had, Magda wanted. Why couldn't his aunt just be satisfied with being herself?

Zmey's shallow, raspy breaths came in spurts. Theo had to do something to speed up the healing process. His father's belt was a twin gift. Magda had said the two combined were more powerful. Theo chided himself for leaving Lamia's at the fortress.

What was I thinking?

But the medallion Theo wore was also a twin gift, at least that was what Magda had said. Since it had been Zunitza's, would it add to the power of Zmey's ouroboros? Theo withdrew the medallion from around his neck and laid it over the ouroboros, willing its power to be infused into Zmey's belt.

The two objects lit and sparked when they met, a soft blue glow emanating from them, expanding along the length of the belt. A gentle breeze caressed Theo's hand, and his mother's voice, tired and weak, spoke to him. *"Thank you."*

Theo held his father's hand, and a healthy color returned to the dragon king's face. As Theo sat there, something Baba Yaga had said bothered him. He turned around to her. "How did you know Magda was gone? How did you know to come here to care for my father, if that's what you really were doing?"

"He he. Ho ho." She hopped around the room, apparently not injured by her contact with the wall. "A little bird told me."

"A little—?" Theo started when Boo poked his head around the corner of the bed.

"Sorry, sorry. Don't be mad." The magpie fluttered closer and nuzzled Theo's shoulder. "I don't like her either, but the Samodivi said the dragon king needed help. They sent me to get the witch."

"How did they know?" Theo asked. "Sava and Ula were with me at Kaleto."

"Kosara saw it in the pond and sent them a message." Boo's head bobbed from side to side as he spoke. "She said there was treachery at the castle and to come quickly."

Theo turned to Baba Yaga and sneered. "So, what's your price to help this time? A place in the royal court? A new chicken hut? A—?"

"Nothing, nothing!" Baba Yaga stomped her way over and stuck her nose in Theo's face. "How many times do I have to tell you to be nice to me? I've done good. I saved you. I saved your human friend. I saved Sitara."

"Yes, but you've always wanted something, a fee, gift, or service, in return for your help." Theo stared her down, despite having to inhale her foul breath. "And often you've tried to take more than was agreed upon."

She snorted. "But this is your father, the king. He's been kind to me. Helped me when no one else would. I wouldn't do anything to harm him."

"But you *have* done things that have harmed Zmey," Theo shouted. "Every time you went running to Lamia or the Youdi, you made things worse for my father."

Baba Yaga lowered her head and backed away, mumbling, "No sense talking with you. You won't understand Zlo's power. Even the witch of witches—that's me—can't deny him his wishes."

"Theo." Zmey's weak voice drew Theo's attention back to his father. "Baba Yaga is my guest. She demands nothing from me. The herbs she brought have kept me alive."

While Theo had been arguing with the witch, his father had begun to revive. A rosy hue brightened his cheeks, the black shadows under his eyes were fading, and his breathing became more even and strong.

"Oh, Father!" Theo grasped Zmey's hand. Strength was returning to his father's grip.

A sparkle had returned to Zmey's eyes. He looked at Theo with love and pride. "Help me up, son."

Theo wound his hands around Zmey's sides. The small wings beneath his father's arms had begun to grow. His father was well on his way to being healed.

Zmey held out his arms, and Theo fell into the embrace. Of all the emotions Theo felt at the moment—grief, joy, anger—the one that overwhelmed him right now was the need to be comforted. He buried his face in Zmey's chest and moaned loudly. For a short time, Theo could be a boy and not a hero. His father was all the family he had left in Zmeykovo. Lamia and Magda were not worthy to be called kin. And Diva and Zunitza were no longer with him, at least not physically. If only he could hold both of them the way he was hugging Zmey. Their warmth and support would comfort him.

"*I am here, my son.*" Zunitza's voice was stronger now. "*I am always with you, even when my strength has weakened.*" A swarm of fireflies materialized and swirled around Theo and Zmey.

Zmey reached out, and they landed on his palm. "Thank you, Theodore and Zunitza." Zmey squeezed Theo tight. "You saved me." Zmey held out one hand to Baba Yaga. "And thank you, my friend, for being here for me."

The witch hobbled over and took the offered hand. "It has been an honor, my king." She scratched her tangled hair. "It appears your son has wounds that should be looked at as well. He is covered in blood."

That did it. Theo broke down and sobbed against Zmey. "It's not mine. It's Diva's. I have some bad news."

Theo's throat constricted and his words came out hoarse. He explained to his father everything that had happened with Magda, how she had stolen Diva as a baby. How Drakus saved Diva. And how she ended up with Sava and Ula.

Zmey lay back against the headboard with his eyes squeezed shut. His grip on Theo tightened as the story unfolded. Finally, the dragon king opened his eyes and said, "I have a daughter? Zunitza, we have a daughter."

Theo gulped. *How am I going to tell Zmey the rest of the story?*

Did his mother already know the truth? If she had been with Theo, even though she hadn't been able to communicate with him, she might. But Zmey didn't, and Theo had to tell him.

"Diva's—" The words stuck in this throat.

Zmey paled. "So much blood. She's injured. Where is Diva now?"

"S-Samodiva Lake. Ula took her there."

"Good, good." Zmey let out a long breath. "The water there can heal her."

"It's too late." Tears flowed freely down Theo's cheeks. He covered his face with both hands. He could share his burden with his father. They could grieve together and support one another. "Lamia k-k-killed Diva. Her own niece. Impaled Diva with that cursed dragon tail."

"Noooo!" Zmey roared.

The castle shook, rattling the windows. Creatures hiding within the walls scratched and skittered away to safety.

Deep lines of sorrow etched Baba Yaga's face, and she touched Zmey's hand. "The Golden Apple can restore her life, but you must act quickly."

"But we don't know where the real one is." Theo ran his fingers through his hair. "I think Diva hid it and gave Lamia the fake one we had Sitara make."

Zmey shook his head slowly. "No. Diva gave Lamia the apple you brought with you from the harvest."

"How? That wasn't the real one."

"No, it wasn't. The Colobari were afraid Lamia would steal the real apple from you." Zmey sighed. "They ordered Kosara to replace it with a fake."

"There were *two* fake apples?"

Zmey nodded.

Theo got up and paced the room, trying to come to terms with what had happened. "You didn't trust me with the real one? You, Kosara, the Colobari. You all thought I would fail?"

"It's not that." Zmey coughed and cleared his throat. "I argued for letting the real apple travel with you, but the Colobari forbade it. You have to remember that the Golden Apple has power over every creature. Everyone has to be considered a suspect, a potential enemy. No one knows exactly what the future holds, not even Kosara. At times, we have to make hard decisions to protect what is valuable. This is why the duplicate apple was created, to lure away the enemy and keep the real one safe."

Zmey's logic made sense. Theo had experienced the apple's pull, its power. Yet still, he felt betrayed. By his own father, who loved him. By Kosara, who said she trusted him. By the Colobari, whom Theo hadn't even met officially. Theo shook off his anger. What was important right now was helping Diva. If the apple could truly bring her back, they had to hurry.

"Then where is the real Golden Apple?" he asked. "We need to bring it to Samodivi Lake immediately."

"It's in the Chamber Room."

"Where is that?"

"Here, in the castle. Follow me." Zmey slipped out of his bed.

With a brisk pace, he led Theo through corridors until they reached the room with the Celestial Turtle carved into the door's panes. It had caught Theo's attention earlier when Magda brought him to meet with Kosara's messengers. He remembered how his fingers had tingled when he'd touched the door. Even though he was still worried about Diva, Theo was excited to be able to find out what was in this room. It was the only door that he'd come across so far that had been locked.

Zmey removed the key from the chain that he wore around his neck. "I'm the only one who has a key to this room. When you inherit my throne, it will be yours." He inserted the key into the lock, flipped it to the left, and then to the right. The lock made a soft click, and Zmey opened the door. "I'm sure you have questions, but for now think of this room as the most valuable archive in our land. A key to secrets and knowledge, the heart of Zmeykovo.”

Inside the room was a box exactly like the one Kosara had given Theo. It rested on a star-shaped table that resembled the seven points of Theo’s medallion. Intricate carvings of dragons and other creatures adorned the exposed areas of the table. A thick layer of dust covered its surface.

Zmey approached the table and lifted the cover on the box.

It was empty.

“Magdaaaaa!” Zmey’s roar shook the castle.

About the Author

Ronesa Aveela is "the creative power of two." Two authors, that is. Nelly, the main force behind the work, the creative genius, was born in Bulgaria and moved to the U.S. in the 1990s. She grew up with stories of wild Samodivi, Kikimora, the dragons Zmey and Lamia, Baba Yaga, and much more. She's a freelance artist and writer. She likes writing mystery romance inspired by legends and tales. In her free time, she paints. Her artistic interests include the female figure, Greek and Thracian mythology, folklore tales, and the natural world interpreted through her eyes. She is married and has two children.

Rebecca, her writing partner was born and raised in the New England area. She has a background in writing and editing, as well as having a love of all things from different cultures. She's learned so much about Bulgarian culture, folklore, and rituals, and writes to share that knowledge with others.

Connect with us at www.ronesaaveela.com.

Be sure to follow us on Kickstarter for extra goodies when we launch new books: https://www.kickstarter.com/profile/ronesa-aveela/.

The Story Concludes …

Discover what happens in the final book of Theo's adventures in *Dragon Village Colobar*: https://books2read.com/DV5-Colobar.

Dragon Village Series

1) *The Unborn Hero of Dragon Village*

2) *Dragon Village Firebird*

3) *Dragon Village Ouroboros*

4) *Dragon Village Golden Apple*

5) *Dragon Village Colobar*

Special Offer

Would you like to learn more about folklore and mythology? Sign up for our newsletter and receive a FREE supplement to our "Spirits and Creatures" book series. To download the article about a malicious water spirit, Vodyanoy or Vodnik, use this link: https://BookHip.com/VFVPQJ or find the link on our website.

Further Reading

Discover more about the dragons and other creatures in this book in our nonfiction series called "Spirits and Creatures." Available in ebook, paperback, and hardcopy formats from your favorite retailer. You can also request your local library to carry a copy.

Household Spirits – https://books2read.com/household-spirits

Rusalki – Slavic Mermaids – https://books2read.com/rusalki

Dragons – https://books2read.com/dragons-aveela

Baba Yaga – https://books2read.com/babayaga

More to come…